"You have me at
a distinct disadvantage, Mel."

She laughed derisively. "Oh, absolutely. This cane is a real threat to a lethal weapon like a . . . gun."

"A gun? Oh, I see. You assume I'm packing a pistol."

She nodded, staring at the many pockets of his pants.

He spread his arms wide. "You won't believe me if I assure you I'm not armed, so why don't you—as they say on television—pat me down? Come on, Mel, don't be shy."

Beginning at her toes, a fiery blush spread through her body with the delirious, fuzzy heat of a fever.

Peter slanted a lazy grin in her direction. "Are you afraid to frisk me, Mel?" he taunted. "A brave woman like you? Surely you can handle any surprises you might find."

For a wildly hallucinatory moment she allowed herself to imagine what it would feel like to run her hands over his magnificent, hard body. A small moan escaped her lips.

In an instant Peter sprang forward, so quickly, so agilely, that he caught her off guard . . .

Hilary Cole

Hilary Cole has enjoyed writing since she was old enough to put pen to paper. She lives with her husband and two sons in Kansas, where she helps run the family furniture business. An avid golfer and enthusiastic spectator of her sons' sporting competitions, she also loves movies—especially romantic comedies of the 1930s and '40s.

Other Second Chance at Love books by
Hilary Cole

THE SWEETHEART TRUST   #290

Dear Reader:

April is a time of warm, wondrous renewal ... and, of course, heady romance. And Christa Merlin begins this month's list of SECOND CHANCE AT LOVE books with her most powerful story ever, *Snowflame* (#328). When Bruce McClure arrives at a mountain hunting lodge, he unexpectedly encounters beautiful Elaine Jeffrey, whose husband has recently been killed in a tragic shooting accident. Beneath Elaine's reserved politeness, Bruce senses her terrible anguish. He can't help offering the comfort he knows she craves ... or prevent passion from surging into sudden, overwhelming love. But he can't accept the agonized words she spills out: that her husband committed suicide — and she could have prevented it! Poignant and compelling, *Snowflame* is a love story that will captivate you from the very first page.

The main ingredient in Diana Morgan's latest romance is pure fun. Take one distraught soap opera writer, Andie Maguire, whose furniture has been abandoned on a New York City sidewalk. Add one handsome but harried efficiency expert, George Demarest, whose cousin has left him with a scruffy toddler. Make the tyke a terrible two-year-old called Speedy, whom Andie agrees to baby-sit — and you've got the zany confection, *Bringing Up Baby* (#329). Don't miss this irresistible romance of hilarious catastrophes and inventive charm.

In *Dillon's Promise* (#330), the ever imaginative Cinda Richards brings you the lovable, roguish, obstinate, utterly unforgettable Scotsman Dillon Cameron. Haunted by a deathbed promise, and shocked to learn that, in a moment of wrenching grief, he fathered a child by his best friend's American widow, Dillon storms Thea Kearney's cottage, intent on claiming "his lasses." But Thea and her baby daughter have little use for such a heart-breaking rover now. Drawing on Scots legends and the magic of the seaswept highlands, Cinda Richards weaves a tale rich in humor, poignancy, and romance.

Next, Hilary Cole returns with *Be Mine, Valentine* (#331), whose Cary Grant-like hero, eccentric supporting cast, and whimsical story line evoke the charm of several silver-screen classics. Heiress Melanie Carroway's unusual family — the butler drinks, and her aunt thinks the dog is her reincarnated lover — fails to prepare her for unconventional thief Peter Valentine. No *ordinary* burglar steals only kisses, gets hired to "protect" his victims, then proceeds to kidnap the boss's daughter! Witty, inventive, and downright funny, *Be Mine, Valentine* is a delightful tale from a writer whose skill is growing by leaps and bounds.

Rarely does a first novel blend lightness and intensity as masterfully as Kit Windham's *Southern Comfort* (#332). The story sounds deceptively simple — Kelly Winters reluctantly agrees to write the script for brash filmmaker Leo Myers's documentary on the Civil War, and travels with him to scout locations — but Kelly and Leo have an appealing complexity that makes for a lively, moving romance. As they dare to share the painful secrets of their pasts, they misunderstand each other in sad, funny, and very human ways that are guaranteed to endear them to every reader. Be one of the first to discover the work of talented Kit Windham, who's sure to be writing many more romances for SECOND CHANCE AT LOVE.

Though not new to readers of romance, Cassie Miles makes her debut at SECOND CHANCE AT LOVE with *No Place for a Lady* (#333), in which heroine Elaine Preston takes a giant step forward for womankind by becoming the first female professional football player. Her teammates remain skeptical, but not robust, insightful Curt Michaels, a former basketball ace who quite literally becomes her staunchest cheerleader! Elaine must go a long way before learning just where she "belongs" — on the field *and* in Curt's arms! — and every step provides thoroughly satisfying romantic entertainment.

With every warm wish that this month's SECOND CHANCE AT LOVE romances will bring a touch of magic into your life...

Ellen Edwards

Ellen Edwards, Senior Editor
SECOND CHANCE AT LOVE
The Berkley Publishing Group
200 Madison Avenue
New York, NY 10016

SECOND CHANCE AT LOVE™

HILARY COLE
BE MINE, VALENTINE

A
SECOND CHANCE AT LOVE
BOOK

For true romantics everywhere
who know
that good sense alone
a lasting relationship
does not make

And for the ladies
of the ball park,
a constant source
of humor and romance

Chapter

1

MELANIE CAUTIOUSLY DESCENDED the stairs, pausing briefly on the last step to lift a hand to her throbbing temple. She'd put off retrieving her headache medication from the kitchen for too long. Although the pain was duller now, it was still persistent, a clear indication that the migraine was not yet giving up. The headaches had come with alarming frequency in the last few months, causing her finally to seek medical advice from a world-famous pain clinic in New Orleans, where she'd spent the last two weeks.

After extensive physical and psychological probing, one of the most esteemed neurologists in the country had diagnosed her headaches as a psychosomatic reaction to stress. He'd recommended that she simply take charge of her life and learn to relax. Tight-lipped, Melanie had accepted the prescription he wrote, paid the exorbitant bill, and returned home to Fort Worth feeling worse than ever.

Dr. What's-His-Name might be an expert in his field, but he hadn't spent thirty years in a family that took to mild insanity the way a duck does to water. Nor did he understand the devastation that had resulted from her one attempt to make a normal life for herself away from her family's insular and slightly demented protection. Taking charge in this household would be a challenge for a marine sergeant! Structure and order were foreign concepts to her family.

As Melanie's slippered feet hit the cold marble floor of the massive downstairs hall, a violent crack of thunder echoed outdoors. Lightning flashed beyond the narrow windows on either side of the front door, and the late-night drizzle suddenly turned into a tempest. Marvelous, Melanie thought tiredly. Just what she needed. Now she had the equivalent of a full orchestra to accompany the tom-toms beating in her head.

She had started toward the kitchen when a scratching noise caught her attention. Warily, she glanced around the hall, then decided a tree branch must be scraping against a window. She took a few more steps, but the nearly imperceptible creaking of a floorboard made her stop once more. Frightened, she glanced toward the library door only a few feet away. Something or someone was in there!

But that was impossible. The mansion and grounds were protected by an elaborate security system, a brace of guard dogs, and an electronic fence. No unauthorized person could possibly be on the premises. She'd barely completed the thought when a dull clinking sound came from the library. Not the tinny noise of rain in the gutter, but more like . . . tumblers on a safe being activated!

Wishing she'd accompanied her father and aunt to the opera, Melanie stared longingly at the telephone in the sitting room across the hall. Did one call the police on such scanty evidence as an over-active imagination, kindled, perhaps, by the violent storm? Certainly not. At least a Carroway didn't. Her family would be outraged if they came home and found uniformed men invading their privacy. On the other hand, what if someone really was cracking the library safe?

Trembling, she stole toward the paneled library door and put her ear to it. There it was again, the sound of movement, followed by a new noise—the indistinct rustle of . . . what? Papers being shuffled? Surely not. Yet . . . she fought the urge to run back up to her room and bolt the door. Then a particularly loud boom of thunder shook the house, and Melanie, perversely encouraged by the danger outside, decided to confront her fears within. After all, they would probably amount to nothing. This was a very old house, subject to the whimsical groans and sighs of any structure its age.

But just to be on the safe side . . . she seized one of her aunt's heavy onyx-handled canes from the umbrella stand in the hall. Taking a deep breath, she cautiously turned the knob and pushed open the library door. A second before her hand hit the master light switch, a dark figure, illuminated momentarily by a zigzag of lightning, whirled to face her.

Melanie screamed and raised the cane over her head, blinking in the suddenly bright light as every lamp in the room came on. The figure in black took one step toward her, then stopped and stood with arms akimbo, a flashlight dangling from one hand, his masked head cocked curiously. "Who the hell are you?" demanded a deeply resonant, decidedly masculine voice.

She was stupefied. In the mystery novels she read, the caught-in-the-act criminal was not the one who did the interrogating. His bold question, plus the discovery that her fears were well-founded, stunned her. She started to answer his question, then paused, trying to control her wobbling knees. "Wait a minute! You have no right to ask me anything! I live here. Just who are you, and what do you think you're doing?"

The man pulled off his black ski mask, shoved it and the flashlight into a pants pocket, and shook his head so that his hair fell back into place. When he took a step toward her, Melanie swung the cane over her head.

"Whoa!" the intruder cautioned. "No need to get violent."

Melanie stopped brandishing her weapon when the man stood very still, perhaps ten feet away from her. "I asked you a question," she said, her voice wavering.

"So you did." He hooked his thumbs in his pockets and appraised her with obvious appreciation.

Melanie stared back at him. He was no more than five feet eleven, she guessed, but his tight black turtleneck sweater and work pants clung to a trim and muscular frame. He made her think of a dangerous predator poised to spring at his prey the moment she let her guard down.

But she had to admit his face wasn't menacing. In fact, his features were open and honest, beginning with the thickly lashed teal-blue eyes, progressing to the aquiline nose, and ending with the lazy slant of his grin. His deep tan suggested he spent a great deal of time outdoors, and bronzed laugh lines softened his generous mouth. He was . . . very attractive. Not classically handsome, but devastatingly charismatic, projecting an aura of sexy confidence. There was something very alive about him that intensified his appeal, making her think not only of strength but of compassion as well.

What in the world was wrong with her? Here she was, holding an intruder at bay with a cane, and her heart was beating not from fear but from . . . an appreciation of his physical attributes! How ridiculous! She wondered what she was going to do if he simply continued to stare back at her with maddeningly apparent amusement. She thrust the cane toward him in what she hoped was a threatening manner. "Who *are* you?" she demanded.

"Ladies before gentlemen—especially beautiful ones," he said firmly. "Who are *you?*"

"*You*'ve broken into *my* house. Tell me who you are and what you're up to immediately, or I'll call the police," Melanie bluffed courageously, knowing she could never get through the door, pick up the phone in the sitting room, and ring the emergency number before he bludgeoned her to death.

The black-garbed intruder laughed huskily, as if he'd read her thoughts. "You're a fiesty woman, aren't you?" He added smoothly, "I'm Peter Valentine, and what I'm doing must be obvious." He folded his arms across his chest. "Satisfied?"

"Is that your real name?" Melanie snapped.

"Cross my heart," Peter answered, tracing an X on his chest with a black-gloved finger. "And may I assume *everything* about you is real as well?" His eyes moved from her face to the generous curves of her breasts beneath her silk robe.

Melanie bit her lip as she flushed hot with embarrassment and indignation.

He laughed again. "Now that I've obliged you, why don't you introduce yourself and tell me what *you*'re doing here?"

Being accustomed to her decidedly strange family, Melanie wasn't all that surprised by his request. Drawing herself up to her full five feet six inches, she said as calmly as possible, "I'm Melanie Carroway, Worth Carroway's daughter, and this is my home—at least for the time being."

Peter ran a hand through his hair, which Melanie noticed was a wonderfully natural silvery blond, and muttered, "Well, I'll be damned!"

"Quite possibly worse than that," she responded dryly, beginning to feel unaccountably relieved. Every instinct was telling her Peter Valentine was not a man to fear, at least not at the moment. "But it might not go so hard on you if you put back everything you've taken from the safe."

He chuckled. "I didn't take anything from the safe—or from anywhere else, for that matter." He raised an eyebrow. "But I'd be delighted to have you search me." He smiled seductively.

Melanie's heartbeat quickened. Outrageous though his suggestion was, it had a certain perverse appeal. Annoyed by her wayward thoughts, she jabbed the cane in the air as if to ward off the magnetism that was drawing her to Peter Valentine.

He threw up his hands in mock surrender, although Melanie suspected he didn't consider her gesture the least bit menacing. "Don't worry, I don't plan on making any moves yet. But I must say I'm tempted. For a blue blood, you're very healthy looking." His eyes traveled slowly down her silk-robed figure. "Hmmm . . . that thick auburn hair appears to be natural, too—skin like alabaster, the biggest brown eyes I've ever seen, nice tilt to the nose, regal throat, magnificent—uh—pectorals, slender waist, long legs . . . in spite of that high-necked robe, you're quite a knockout."

Embarrassment colored her cheeks. The situation was

entirely out of hand! "You," she began in a rigid tone, "have an uncommon amount of gall. Especially for a burglar!"

Peter Valentine laughed softly, then fixed her with an imperturbable gaze. "I have to admire your courage, Mel. Except for that one shrill scream when you first discovered me, you've held your ground damned well."

Melanie glared at him. "I don't need compliments from a . . . a common burglar. And my name is not Mel."

He tilted his head disarmingly, breaking into a husky, improvised lyric: "Well, darlin', you'll always be Mel to me." As a finale he removed his gloves with a flourish and tucked them into yet another pants pocket.

Nothing in Melanie's background had prepared her for a singing burglar! Drawing on what was left of her sanity, she said coolly, "Mr. Valentine, I'm going to call the police."

"It'll be embarrassing for you," he warned.

"For *me!*"

He nodded emphatically. "Absolutely. Don't you think you ought to interrogate me some more first? When you have the facts, you may decide you don't want to take any action."

Peter slouched lazily against the elaborate Louis XV desk, shoving his hands into his pockets and crossing his ankles. Melanie couldn't help noticing how the tightly drawn fabric of his pants emphasized his lean, powerfully muscled thighs. Here was a man who kept himself in extremely good shape. One, no doubt, who was capable of demonstrating surprising strength if the occasion demanded. "Why don't you let me ask some questions first, and then it'll be your turn," he suggested brightly.

"You're stalling," Melanie pointed out.

"Perhaps," he admitted, "but fair is fair. Now, I've never heard of you, so for starters, why don't you tell me why you're here tonight?"

This was the most incredibly ridiculous situation! What in the world was she doing, standing in her robe, allowing herself to be questioned by a cat burglar? Even if he was the most compelling man she'd ever met, she should have followed her instincts and called for help. But perhaps if she played along with him, her father, aunt, and Brown would arrive home, and she could call out when she heard the front door open. That was probably her best chance, although her fear was rapidly being replaced by intense curiosity.

"Well," she began slowly, "I'm home tonight because I had a headache and didn't want to go to the opera with the rest of them."

"Your father, aunt, and who else?" Peter demanded, a quizzical expression shadowing the lean planes and angles of his face.

"Uh, Brown, our butler."

An eyebrow shot up. "Your butler accompanies the family to the opera?"

"He loves it."

"What a liberal bunch you are!"

"Well, Brown's been with the family for years, and he's..." How could she explain Brown? "He's more one of us than a servant."

Peter nodded gravely. "My people told me this was an eccentric household."

"Your people? My God, are you part of a ring or something?" Melanie's hand flew to her throat.

Peter laughed delightedly. "Sort of," he admitted. "But what puzzles me is that no one mentioned *you*. After all, a beautiful young woman is definitely worth discussing. I was told about the servants, of course, but I figured they'd be no problem. Servants usually find very engrossing ways to occupy themselves when their employers are out. But *you*'re definitely a problem. Actually a rather delightful one. Nevertheless, I'm going to have to berate my men for their lack of thoroughness."

"So, you're the *leader?*" Melanie asked warily.

"Right," Peter affirmed. His eyes wandered over a Ming vase on the desk and returned to her in an appraisal so intense that Melanie's heart went into a faster rhythm. "I want to make sure I have all my facts straight, Mel, so I won't ever make this kind of mistake again. I can't stand shoddy work."

Her lower jaw was falling open. Good Lord, this man,

this criminal, was practicing his burglary technique on her! He was much more dangerous than she'd thought. Better continue to play along with him, stall for time until she got a chance to make her move.

"You weren't living here two weeks ago," Peter said thoughtfully.

She shook her head. "I've been in New Orleans for . . . a vacation of sorts." No point in telling him the whole truth, she decided. Peter Valentine didn't look like a man who'd ever had a stress headache in his life, and she certainly couldn't expect him to understand the real reason for her absence. "I returned home today. I'll be staying here until . . . until I decide exactly what to do next."

"Must be nice to have the leisure in which to make those decisions," he returned without bitterness. "I've had to work so damned hard learning my trade that I haven't had any spare time in years. But things have been going very well lately. In fact, before long I may be able to take a vacation."

"Considering the business you're in, Mr. Valentine, I'm sure the prosperous citizens of Fort Worth will be grateful," she said fiercely.

He gave a dry chuckle. "Actually, Mel, those prosperous citizens of whom you speak will be the first to miss my presence, believe me."

"What a ridiculous assumption!" Melanie rejoined. "Do you actually think people want someone like you on the loose?"

He smiled knowingly. "Come here, Mel," he said huskily. Then, in even deeper tones, "Don't make me beg you. Just walk on over here. I promise you won't be disappointed."

She shrank back against the solid wood door. Oh, good Lord, had she really angered him this time? She watched him carefully, half expecting him to whip out a gun.

"Please, Mel," he entreated, his voice tinged with amusement.

He was actually enjoying this, she realized. Peter Valentine was a sadist! "No," she said in a cracked voice that bore no resemblance to her own.

He took a few steps toward her. Melanie raised the cane. He stopped. "You have me at a distinct disadvantage, Mel."

She laughed derisively, forgetting for a moment the terrible danger she was in. "Oh, absolutely. This cane is a real threat to a lethal weapon like a . . . gun."

"A gun? Oh, I see. You assume I'm packing a pistol."

She nodded, staring at the many pockets in his pants, wondering which one held the firearm.

He spread his arms high and wide. "You won't believe me if I assure you I'm not armed, so why don't you—as they say on television—pat me down?" When she still made no move toward him, he planted his feet several inches apart and smiled tantalizingly. "Come on, Mel, don't be shy. Too bad you don't have any handcuffs. If I were shackled, you'd feel perfectly safe while searching my body to your heart's content." There was no mistaking his sexual innuendo.

"Really," she said haughtily, unable to tear her gaze from his blue eyes.

He shrugged. "Could be fun. Kinky, of course, but droll. Come on, Mel, search me. Imagine your delight when you find my concealed weapon."

Beginning at her toes, a fiery blush spread through her body with the delirious, fuzzy heat of a fever. She nearly dropped the cane. What had started out as embarrassment and indignation was rapidly turning into a free-for-all for her galloping libido. How could this be happening?

Peter slanted a lazy grin in her direction. "Are you afraid to frisk me, Mel?" he taunted in a voice that could melt icicles. "A brave woman like you? Surely you can handle any surprises you might find."

For a wildly hallucinatory moment she allowed herself to imagine what it would feel like to run her hands over his magnificent, hard body. A small moan escaped her lips. She blinked, trying to dispel the erotic image.

Peter took advantage of her hesitation. "You could start at the top of my head, Mel, and work your way down. If it'd make you feel better, I'd even allow you to remove my clothing, garment by garment." His velvety tones were smoothly enticing. Unconsciously, Melanie took a small step toward him, drawn like a moth to the flame. Then reason suddenly took over. The man was a master at seduction! How many other women had he conned into handing over their valuables as he caressed them with his voice, his hands . . .

"This is no joking matter," Melanie retorted angrily.

His eyes softened in pretended sympathy. "I can see that to you it most assuredly isn't." Slowly, his hands dropped to his sides, and his expression turned serious. "This isn't a joking matter to me either, Mel. And I think, deep down, you really know that, don't you?"

Melanie's lips parted slightly. The attraction between them was so compelling that she felt as if she were in a force field, being magnetically pulled toward the irresistible object that was Peter Valentine. Her fingers relaxed on the cane, which dangled limply in her hand as she swayed slightly.

In an instant Peter sprang forward, so quickly, so agilely, that he caught Melanie off guard. Somehow he managed to wrest the cane from her, throw it to one side, and envelop her in his arms all at once. She opened her mouth to scream but realized no sound was coming forth. As his strong arms crushed her against him, she was all too aware of the flimsy protection offered by her thin robe. Pinning both of her arms to her sides, he tilted up her chin and covered her lips with his own.

The kiss was intense, but not punishing. She tried to throw her head back, but the hand on her chin moved to the nape of her neck, catching the shiny spill of hair. The breath went out of her as Peter Valentine moved his mouth over hers in a wonderfully nonthreatening manner, though she couldn't have escaped if she'd tried.

When he finally released her, she sagged against the door, breathing raggedly, her lips trembling. He smiled. "Now that we're more intimately acquainted, Mel, I want to show you something."

Speechless, she allowed him to propel her toward the wall safe. For the first time she noticed that the door was slightly ajar. How had he managed to crack it without setting off the alarms? Still keeping his hold on her, he pushed the door wide open and gestured for her to look inside.

She peered into the safe. All of the jewelry, cash, and important papers appeared to be untouched. On top of a single strand of rubies and pearls in a transparent plastic storage bag lay a white business card. She looked questioningly at him.

"Read it," he said firmly.

Tentatively, she picked up the card and read it aloud: "Peter Valentine, Security Analyst. We protect you and yours." A phone number, address, and a short list of specialties followed, but Melanie barely glanced at them. "I— I don't understand..." She faltered, lifting her face to his.

His sea-colored eyes flickered. "Correction. You *didn't* understand. Surely you do now."

"You mean you're not a thief?" she mumbled.

"I'm on the other side," he admitted wryly. "I don't wear a white hat or a badge, but I'm bonded. Is that good enough?"

He was making fun of her again. Anger and relief replaced the last vestiges of her fear. She jerked free of his grasp and thrust a finger into his face. "Why didn't you tell me this immediately? And how did you get in here? Who hired you? What is this card doing *inside* the safe if you're not a thief? Why are you dressed like some damned cat burglar? And—"

"That's too many questions for a thirsty man to answer. Tell you what. Why don't we sit down with a snifter of your father's good brandy, and I'll be more in the mood to clear up every little detail."

Unaccountably she had a feeling that if she refused, he might disappear into thin air, taking that magnificent body and her unanswered questions with him. "All right," she agreed. "But I warn you that I expect the complete truth."

She was rewarded with a dazzling smile. "Absolutely."

Melanie walked to the leather-covered bar and, with a shaky hand, poured brandy into two crystal snifters. What in the world had she gotten herself into? For a woman who led a fairly predictable, sometimes downright boring life, this evening was like a scene from *Alice in Wonderland*. But she actually felt exhilarated. And her headache had disappeared!

Peter had settled into a Louis XV chair. One leg dangled over the curved arm, and his arm was curled casually around the tapestry-upholstered back. Melanie had never seen anyone defile a period piece by sitting in such an unorthodox manner. That particular chair had come from France, was an exquisite example of eighteenth-century craftsmanship, and worth more than most people made in a year.

She handed Peter a snifter and sat primly across from him in a cabriole-legged chair decorated with carved lions' heads. He made a show of swirling the amber-colored liquid in his glass and swigged down a hefty amount in one gulp.

Pointedly, Melanie took a dainty sip of her own drink and fixed him with a quelling stare. Peter ignored the putdown and just kept raising his glass to his lips until it was empty. He set the snifter on a Chippendale table. "Just what I needed," he proclaimed. "Something else to warm the cockles of my heart."

Melanie raised questioning eyebrows.

"You warmed me first with your kiss," he explained mischievously.

"It was not *my* kiss." She averted her gaze. "I did not *ask* to be kissed," she said in her best finishing school tones.

"You didn't protest either."

"How in the world could I?" she cried, accidentally sloshing some brandy onto her robe. "You've got arms and legs like steel."

"The result of years spent leaping tall buildings in a single bound."

"I wouldn't put your occupation in the same league as Superman's."

"That just goes to show that you need to learn more about what I do for a living."

"I'm listening," she replied stiffly.

"Yes, and I've already drunk my bribe for telling you what you want to know, haven't I? Time to begin, I guess. Let's see, if memory serves me, you first asked why I didn't correct your impression of me immediately after you caught me at my dastardly deed."

"Yes."

"You didn't give me a chance at first, and then I thought

if I told you the truth, you might dismiss me as you would a servant and disappear from my life forever." As the light from the candlestick lamp caught his eyes, Melanie realized they were a multitude of different shades—green, blue, gold, even a hint of gray. Mesmerizing eyes, the kind a woman could lose herself in. "I didn't want to risk that," Peter continued. "You're fascinating, Mel. There's a gorgeously seductive quality about you, yet you have an innocent appeal. You're spunky and brave, but you're afraid of something. Maybe of taking a chance on life? Or love? I want to know why someone like you would fear either. And what chance I might have of making you change your mind . . ."

Melanie inhaled sharply, alarmed to feel her heart pound entirely too fast in response to his words. She'd had little doubt that their attraction was mutual, but to hear Peter speak so directly was unsettling. She must lead him back to safer topics. "Well, how did you get in here? We have what I thought was a foolproof security system."

His hand wagged in a so-so motion. "It's too complicated to explain fully, but in simple terms I bypassed the electronic surveillance system that controls the locks, the fence, and the alarms."

"But what about the dogs?"

"They're enjoying a peaceful high. I just tossed them each a chunk of liver with a specially developed pet tranquilizer in it and waited a few minutes before I scaled the fence. Your father knew the dogs could be handled easily, but he didn't think I could throw a wrench in your electronic system."

Melanie nodded dazedly. "And the safe?"

He reached into a below-the-knee pants pocket, withdrew a small electronic gadget, and held it up for her inspection. "This gizmo, and some other secrets of the trade, helped me open it. Dressed in black on a dark, rainy night, with the alarm system out of commission, I entered easily through that window and opened the safe in a matter of seconds— a perfectly executed operation, until you burst onto the scene."

Melanie's thought processes seemed to have been short-circuited by the distressing information Peter had just shared.

"But I don't understand why Father didn't tell me your break-in was going to take place tonight. He could have alerted me to—"

"He didn't know when I was coming. I tell all my clients I'll check things out when they least expect it. That's the way a real thief operates, and I like to keep my little forays as close as possible to the real thing. All your father knew was that I'd have a report for him within a month of our first conference. I always leave my card when I break in, to prove that I've actually penetrated the security system."

Melanie sank back into the chair. "Oh." She leaned forward almost immediately as his real message sank in. "But what can we do about the failure of our security system? We can't go unprotected. I mean, if *you* can break in, then who knows—"

Pretending to take offense, Peter feigned a dismayed expression. "Bite your tongue, Mel! It'd take a better-than-ordinary criminal to do what I've just done." He swung his leg off the arm of the chair and leaned forward to rest both elbows on his knees. "Admittedly, there are some highly competent criminals who are as good as I am at my job—particularly jewel thieves and kidnappers. Those types really know the ropes. So, I'll make certain specific recommendations to your father when we have our conference."

He was still staring unabashedly at her. Distracted, she managed to ask, "Such as?"

He stood up, his thigh muscles rippling as he stretched onto his toes, his heels slamming back down onto the carpet with a resounding thud. She sensed his restless energy as clearly as if they'd touched. He answered her question forcefully, his hot gaze burning into her. "Until the security system's updated, however, I intend to be your personal bodyguard twenty-four hours a day."

Melanie gasped.

He crossed to her chair in three steps, pressed the heels of his hands on the arms of her chair, and leaning over her, his face only inches from hers, said out of the corner of his mouth, in the husky, tough tones of Bogart, "It's a dirty job, Mel, but somebody's got to do it."

Chapter

2

"YOU CAN'T BE SERIOUS," Melanie exclaimed, tilting her head slightly to escape his disturbing nearness. In spite of her flushed skin, shivers assailed her spine, and her heart had resumed its version of the cha-cha.

"I'm becoming more serious by the moment," Peter assured her.

"That's perfectly ridiculous. I have no intention of allowing my every move to be observed."

Peter flashed a quirky grin. "Why? Do you have something to hide? A boyfriend of whom Papa wouldn't approve, perhaps?"

Melanie leaned forward in a burst of outrage and bumped right into his nose. Immediately, she sat back. "I—the men—man, I mean . . . they're—he's perfectly acceptable to my father, let me assure you. Furthermore—" A thought interrupted her words. "How do you know I'm not married?"

His all-knowing smile reappeared quickly. "You're still living in your father's house, you haven't mentioned a husband, and you're not wearing a wedding ring. Put them all together, they spell 'single,' Mel." He cast another sizzling glance over the length of her. "I can't imagine how someone as lovely as you could have escaped matrimony this long."

"What do you mean, 'this long'? I'm not exactly over the hill."

"Hey, did I say that? What I meant is, I can't imagine your being single much past the age of twenty-two. On the other hand, the rich, I'm told, often take their time, hoping to marry well." Peter cocked his head disarmingly. "How old are you, Mel?"

Icily, she replied, "A gentleman never asks a lady's age."

Peter shrugged. "I haven't promised to be a gentleman. And if we're going to spend a lot of time together, I need to know all of your vital statistics."

"We are *not,* I repeat *not* going to be spending a lot of time together," she corrected firmly. "I do *not* need a body-guard."

"There's been a rash of kidnappings in the area lately, Mel, and when I tell your father about them, I think—"

"Kidnappings!"

"Hmmm . . . now, how old are you?"

She clenched her teeth, trying not to meet his mocking eyes. "If I tell you my age, will you let me up out of this chair?"

"I guess that's a fair trade," he agreed, bending still closer.

She could feel his warm breath on her face, smell the rain-fresh scent of his clothes mixed with a clean, soapy fragrance. "Thirty," she announced, hoping he didn't notice the pounding pulse at the base of her throat.

"No kidding! I would have guessed you to be younger— maybe twenty-seven."

"Thanks, I think," she retorted dryly. "Now, will you please move so I can get out of this chair?"

"I'm twenty-eight."

"Well, you're not going to live to see my age if you don't get out of my way."

"Mel, Mel . . . is that any way for a lady to talk?" he chastised playfully.

"I mean it, Mr. Valentine."

"Peter. If you call me Peter, I'll definitely move."

She swallowed hard. "Peter," she repeated faintly. Just

saying his name aloud provoked disturbing thoughts of intimacy.

He stepped back, but when Melanie stood up, she suddenly found herself in Peter Valentine's arms. He pulled her against the hard length of his body, setting her every pulse point on fire. A delicious tremor shuddered through her, and it took all of her willpower to utter an indignant "Peter!"

"I said I'd move, but I didn't say in what direction," he pointed out. "I have some very important questions to ask you, and they're best answered in this position—what I call a getting-to-know-you embrace."

"One in which you've obviously had a great deal of practice," Melanie retorted, wondering why that idea disturbed her.

Not bothering to confirm or deny her assumption, Peter rubbed his nose against hers and asked softly, "Did you chew bubble gum when you were a kid?"

She attempted to bring her hands up to push him back, but without the merest hint of force, he simply pinned her arms securely to her waist. "What does my chewing bubble gum have to do with anything?"

"I'm trying to find out if they had bubble gum when you were a kid."

"How insulting! Of course, they had bubble gum. I'm not *that* old."

"Ah, so we do have something in common. I chewed bubble gum, too."

"Bully for you," she replied half angrily. "Please let me go."

"Do you remember the big band era?"

"I wasn't even born yet, and you know it."

"Great. Neither was I."

"This is the most inane conversation. Release me."

"In a minute."

Melanie sighed. A couple more minutes in Peter Valentine's arms, and she was going to dissolve into a pool on the floor.

"Do you like anchovies on pizza?"

"Well, yes, as a matter of fact."

He stepped back in surprise. "Perfect!"

"Perfect?" she repeated, still confused by the stirring sensations his embrace had created. Her cheeks felt flushed, and her stomach felt woozy.

"Wait!" Peter exclaimed, snapping his fingers. "I forgot one last but very important question. If you were stranded on a desert island, what would you wish for the most?"

Melanie walked straight to the bar and poured herself another brandy. She took an enormous swallow. "Rescue," she answered acidly.

"Interesting," Peter murmured, joining her in another drink. "Most people, when asked that question, think in terms of passing the time pleasantly. You know, they wish for a year's supply of chocolate bars, or their favorite movie star to be shipwrecked with them—things like that."

Melanie rubbed a temple and braced one foot on the brass rail below the bar to steady herself. "Why are you asking for this silly information?"

"Because," Peter said smugly, "I want to know what we have in common. Which, by the way, turns out to be a lot. You don't remember the big band era, and neither do I. We both chewed bubble gum, and we both like anchovies on pizza. Last, and perhaps most significant, when I was asked the desert-island question, I gave the same answer you did. As I said before, perfect."

Melanie stared at him. "That trivia establishes absolutely nothing of any real value."

"On the contrary. It's obvious that in spite of the slight gap between our ages and the much greater difference in our social status, we're meant for each other."

"You're insane."

In a lightning-swift move, he took her glass, set it next to his, and kissed her—before she could even blink.

He was *not* a novice kisser. She felt as if she had a temperature every time he touched her. And this was the most bizarre thing that had ever happened to her!

The kiss deepened, and Melanie's arms involuntarily circled Peter's neck. Even as the pressure of her lips on his grew more demanding, she reminded herself that she must be out of her mind to be kissing a stranger—and enjoying it! Sensible people just didn't do this kind of thing. Then Peter's mouth moved to the slender column of her throat, scorching the delicate flesh with searing intensity.

The last rational thought flew from her head. She was drowning in his arms, going down for the third time, and she had absolutely no desire to come back up again . . .

The sound of the front door opening startled both of them out of the embrace. Melanie staggered slightly, but Peter's hand caught her. For one interminable moment, as voices mingled in the hallway, they stood breathlessly gazing into each other's eyes. Finally Melanie summoned the willpower to lower her gaze. Hastily, she readjusted her robe and pushed back the dark red hair cascading around her face. "They're home," she said shakily.

"I love kissing you," Peter pronounced huskily. "You taste good, like brandy, and you smell like roses, and your skin is like flower petals."

Melanie's trembling legs at last made a connection with the master control panel in her brain, and she managed to move past him to open the library door. "Hi," she said in a voice she didn't recognize.

Her father, Aunt Maddie, and Brown were hanging their raincoats on the hall tree. A large brown dog stood behind them, shaking moisture from his shaggy fur. "Hullo, darling," Worth Carroway greeted her, coming over to kiss her cheek. "Headache better?"

She nodded mutely. Her father smiled in satisfaction, then turned to put his umbrella in the stand.

Aunt Maddie smiled vaguely in Melanie's general direction, leaning heavily on her marble-handled cane. "Wonderful," she proclaimed. "Everything was divine, except for this foul weather." She looked up at the ancient, thin butler who was holding her elbow, whether for her support or his own, it was hard to tell. "Isn't that true, Brown?"

"Quite, madam." He frowned. "Do you have a guest, Melanie?"

"Uh, why do you ask, Brown?"

The butler's lips compressed. "Because there's a man

dressed all in black standing directly behind you."

Melanie whirled around. Peter was lounging against the door frame, smiling expectantly. "Hello," he said casually, as if he'd just arrived for dinner.

Worth Carroway peered nearsightedly at Peter, and fumbled in his tuxedo jacket for his glasses. "Who's this?" he muttered. "That isn't Harris's voice, is it? What have I done with my confounded glasses?"

"Right here, sir," Brown answered smoothly, withdrawing them from his own pocket. "And in answer to your question, the gentleman is not Mr. Mortimer."

"Who's Harris Mortimer?" Peter asked.

"Melanie's most loyal suitor," Aunt Maddie chirped, leaning heavily on her cane as she moved toward Peter. "My, you're a handsome young man. Who are you?"

Peter took the older woman's hand and bent to kiss it. "Peter Valentine, madam. I've been waiting for Mr. Carroway to arrive home so that I could speak to him about business. In the meantime, your niece has kept me charmingly entertained."

Aunt Maddie frowned. "Darling, you should have worn a tea gown. Bathrobes are not for entertaining. Remember your finishing school training."

"I wasn't expecting company, Aunt dear," Melanie said unevenly, beginning to feel a suspicious throbbing in her temples.

Worth Carroway, who had managed to jam his spectacles onto his nose, suddenly snapped his fingers. "You're Peter Valentine! From the security organization! How nice of you to drop by on such a despicable night."

"Father," Melanie began slowly, "why didn't you tell me about Mr. Valentine? He caught me by—uh—surprise."

"Sorry, love. Must have slipped my mind. I've been so delightfully preoccupied with your homecoming, you see." He rubbed his hands together briskly. "Well, no harm done, I'm sure. Let's go into the library and have a drink."

"McNurty could have his in the kitchen just this once, couldn't he, Aunt Maddie?" Melanie pleaded, eyeing the enormous bedraggled dog.

Her aunt regarded her in surprise. "What on earth for, dear? He always has cocktails with us, Melanie."

"I know. I just thought since we have a guest—"

"Oh!" Aunt Maddie turned to Peter. "Mr. Valentino, I'm afraid I've been dreadfully rude by not properly introducing McNurty to you." She fondled the dog's head.

"I wasn't aware the household had any pets other than the guard dogs outside," Peter said.

"Oh, McNurty's not a *pet,*" Aunt Maddie corrected.

"Aunt—" Melanie began desperately.

"He's not?" Peter asked.

"Certainly not. Or at least not in the usual sense. You see, Mr. Valentino, McNurty's the reincarnation of my dead lover, Harold McNurty."

Melanie raised a hand to her throbbing forehead, not daring to glance at Peter.

"How interesting," he returned.

"Yes," Aunt Maddie agreed happily. "You see, Harold McNurty, the love of my life, died in the explosion of the *Hindenburg*. It was in all the papers."

"I've heard about the disaster," Peter answered smoothly.

"Terrible tragedy." Aunt Maddie sighed. "We were engaged to be married, Mr. Valentino. The wedding was only a few days away when Harold was killed. Naturally, I was grief-stricken. My youngest sister, Caroline, Melanie's mother, insisted I come live with her family until I recovered. Well, I never have, so I'm still here." She fondly stroked the dog's ears. "But ever since McNurty showed up on our doorstep I've been able to cope with my sorrow."

"When was that?" Peter asked with interest. "I mean, how long has McNurty been living here?"

"He first arrived in 1948," Aunt Maddie replied. "Just showed up on the doorstep one day. Providential."

Melanie smiled brightly. "Yes, well, let's see. About the drinks—"

"That makes McNurty somewhat of a biological miracle, then," Peter concluded. "I've never known a dog to live so long."

"Not really, Mr. Valentino. You see, this is the fifth

McNurty I've had in all these years. Soon after the first one passed on, another showed up, and so on and so on . . . Providential, as I said."

"Keeps Maddie as happy as she can be, under the circumstances," Worth Carroway interjected somberly.

"That's wonderful," Peter said. "I'd be very interested in hearing, madam, exactly how you knew that McNurty . . . was McNurty."

"No!" Melanie cried. Every head swiveled toward her curiously. "I mean not until after we have drinks," she explained feebly.

"Quite right, darling," her father agreed. "I always enjoy chatting, but I do it so much better if I'm sitting down."

All five of them settled into chairs. Peter chose one directly across from Melanie, who sat next to her aunt. McNurty lay at the older woman's feet, gazing up at her with abject devotion.

"Brown," Worth Carroway said, "could you please see to some refreshments?"

The butler looked at him solemnly. "I doubt it, sir. My arthritis, you know."

Melanie's father nodded. Melanie couldn't help glancing at Peter to gauge his reaction. He was smiling lopsidedly, apparently enjoying the situation. He hadn't seen anything yet!

"Where's Cora?" Aunt Maddie demanded.

"Maid's night out, madam," Brown explained, removing his patent-leather opera pumps to massage his feet. "Cook's, too."

"I'll take care of refreshments," Melanie interjected quickly, knowing that in a moment her father would be waiting on them all if she didn't.

"How sweet." Aunt Maddie sighed. "Don't forget McNurty, dear."

Melanie hurried to the bar and began to set out drinks on a sterling serving tray. Her hands shook as she heard her aunt say clearly, "Now, Mr. Valentino, tell me again what it is you do."

"I'm a security analyst, madam. Your entire system, I'm

afraid, needs upgrading. I'm here to make a full report to Mr. Carroway."

"Good," her aunt declared. "I can't stand the thought of anyone breaking in here and disturbing our privacy, Mr. Valentino. We like to keep to ourselves, you know."

"Yes," Peter answered. "I can well imagine."

Distractedly, Melanie flew around the room, serving the drinks. As she handed Brown his, he looked at her disapprovingly. "You've forgotten my twist of lemon."

"Sorry," she apologized. "I'll get it in a minute."

She served Peter last. As she bent over with the heavy tray, he whispered, "Are you serious about this Harris person?"

"Very," she hissed back, making a swift retreat to get the forgotten twist.

She was back in seconds, dropped the lemon in Brown's king-sized drink, and scurried into her chair, where she reasoned she might be in a better position to control the situation. The instant she sat down, McNurty let out a baleful howl. Aunt Maddie patted her spray of frizzy white curls. "Melanie darling, I hate to mention it again, but you did forget McNurty."

"Oh, Lord," Melanie muttered under her breath. Smiling sweetly, she rose once more, mixed bourbon and water in a sterling bowl, and placed it on the floor in front of the dog. McNurty slurped eagerly as Aunt Maddie watched approvingly.

Melanie collapsed back into her chair, caught Peter's intense gaze, and began fanning herself with a cocktail napkin. "It seems so warm in here," she gasped.

"Your cheeks do look flushed," her aunt commented. "As a matter of fact, you have the same glow I always had when Harold was . . . Harold. Are you in love, Melanie?"

Across from her, Peter choked on his drink. Fixing him with a piercing, dark stare, Melanie smiled radiantly. "No, dear. It's stuffy in here."

"Well, don't open the windows," Brown demanded peevishly. "I'm liable to catch a chill, and that's not good for my arthritis."

"If only Harold had lived longer, he could have been killed in the invasion of Normandy on D day. Then I would have been a war hero's widow," Aunt Maddie said wistfully.

"Fate's such a fickle creature," Peter agreed sympathetically.

Melanie shot him a warning look, which he returned with an innocent smile.

"Mr. Valentine," Worth Carroway began in his Texas gentleman's drawl, "I'm most eager to learn of your findings. Would you begin, please?"

"Certainly, sir. I'll be as brief as possible."

Brown sighed heavily. "Thank you, young man. We've had a long night. I'm exhausted. I had to leave the opera three times to fetch McNurty from the limo. Confounded driver refused to walk him."

Peter nodded pleasantly, as if the butler's complaints were part of the natural order of things. "The guard dogs were no problem, Mr. Carroway, as you already had surmised. And I found it almost as easy to bypass your electronic surveillance system. Do you realize you're not even hooked up to the police department?"

Aunt Maddie clapped her hands together. "Oh, my! We used to be, but I was always accidentally setting that silly alarm off, and then the police would come—such a nuisance. I had the company who installed the system disconnect that part quite some time ago."

"I didn't know," Worth Carroway mused.

Peter cleared his throat. "The safe was a piece of cake, too. It's outmoded. Extensive changes are needed in your entire system of protection devices. Also, I think you need a man to keep an eye on things around here until that's all accomplished. Especially on these lovely ladies, Mr. Carroway. As I was telling your daughter earlier, there have been several kidnappings in the area lately, and until these criminals are caught, it's better to be safe than sorry. You're really quite vulnerable right now, what with your estate being outside the city limits and your security system being so easy to penetrate."

In the confusion, Melanie had nearly forgotten about

Peter's intention to be her bodyguard. Quickly, she said, "Father, I agree with Mr. Valentine about the electronic security devices, but I don't think—"

Her father shook his silver head authoritatively. "Now, now, darling, let's not pretend to know more than Mr. Valentine. He came highly recommended, and I plan to do everything he suggests. Why, if anything were to happen to you, or to your mother's dear sister"—he inclined his head in Aunt Maddie's direction—"I'd simply never forgive myself. My desire to protect our property is secondary to my concern about your safety."

"I knew *you'd* see it my way, sir," Peter replied pointedly.

Melanie avoided looking at him. "Father," she pleaded, "I haven't read about any kidnappings—"

"They don't usually publicize that kind of thing," Peter interrupted. "But my firm is aware of some recent occurrences."

"Absolutely," Worth Carroway agreed. "Only encourages that riffraff if they see attention paid to their foul deeds in the media. And, of course, my love, you've been in Europe until recently."

"Oh?" Peter asked innocently.

Before Melanie could respond, her aunt chimed in. "Yes, our dear Melanie finally came home to finish recovering from her terrible tragedy."

"No," Peter protested dramatically. "You don't say."

"Aunt Maddie—" Melanie interjected.

"I do say," the older woman declared. She leaned forward conspiratorially. "Mr. Valentino, Melanie was taken in by a fortune hunter. She'd been married to him for several months before the truth came out." She shook her head sadly. "Terrible, terrible. But at least the divorce is now final."

"I hardly think—" Melanie began.

"How awful," Peter commiserated, but she heard the smugness in his voice. "I'll have to screen every one of her suitors, then, won't I?"

"Yes," her father agreed. "Good idea. Even that old boy, Harris. People, Mr. Valentine, often claim to be of respectable background when in fact it's all a masquerade. Not like the old days when one knew every family in town for what they really were." He arched a heavy white brow disapprovingly.

"Exactly," Peter replied. "Charlatans come in all disguises nowadays."

"You can say that again," Melanie muttered.

Peter shot her a playfully reproving glance, which no one else seemed to notice.

Brown shakily held up his glass. He was, Melanie realized, clearly on his way to his usual inebriated state. "Empty," he complained.

"I'll get it," Peter offered. He rose to take the butler's glass and mix him another drink. Melanie closed her eyes briefly. What a nightmare this evening was turning into! Brown was going to fall right out of his chair if he had much more to drink, and now her father and aunt had just approved Peter's plan to guard her!

"Can you spare your best man for all of this security business, Mr. Valentine?" her father asked sternly as Peter handed Brown another large drink.

"As it happens, Mr. Carroway, I myself am available. And I'll gladly lend my services for the next few weeks. Everything should be cleared up by then." He smiled reassuringly at Melanie. "Completely resolved," he added conclusively.

"Wonderful!" her father boomed. "I've put all of this off much too long. My lawyer's been after me for ages, but I was reluctant to have a stranger know our business. Until he checked into your firm—discreetly, of course—and told me of your impeccable reputation." Worth Carroway tented his fingers, peering at Peter over his spectacles. "Now, when can you start?"

"Tomorrow. I'll need to live in, sir, if that's satisfactory."

"Indeed."

"I don't think Cora's cleaned any of the guest rooms in the east wing," Brown slurred. "Such a lazy twit."

McNurty emitted a loud burp and rolled onto his back.

"Where do Melanie and her aunt sleep?" Peter asked.

"Wait a minute—" Melanie protested.

"We're both in the west wing, but a long hall separates our rooms," Aunt Maddie supplied cheerfully.

"Fine. I'll choose a room in the middle."

Everyone but Melanie and Brown nodded in satisfaction. She was too stunned, and he was too intoxicated. The empty glass rolled from his hand onto the Persian rug with a soft thud as his head slumped forward.

"Oh, my," Aunt Maddie lamented, "Brown's taken too much medicine again. You know, he had several toddies at intermission."

Worth Carroway nodded gravely. "Poor man. He's an invaluable servant, but his arthritis causes him to imbibe more than he should to control the pain."

McNurty burped again and threw a large paw over his eyes.

Melanie slid down in her chair. Well, she told herself, at least things couldn't get much worse.

"I'll be glad to carry Brown to his room," Peter offered. "He's plainly exhausted."

"Oh, that's not necessary, Mr. Valentino," Aunt Maddie said, smiling. "Just get him to the chair lift. We use it all the time to take him upstairs when he's ill. I use the confounded thing, too, because of my heart, you know."

"Quite," Peter replied in a perfect imitation of Brown.

Melanie groaned aloud. Was she the only one who could see that Peter was having fun at their expense?

"Darling!" her father exclaimed. "Is your headache worse?"

"Awful." She sighed. "Absolutely awful."

"I'm sorry, lamb. You must go to bed and try to rest."

"Tell you what, Mr. Carroway," Peter said. "Just let me assist Brown to his room, and then I'll return to help your daughter to hers. I wouldn't want her to faint from the pain of the migraine. She could fall down the stairs and injure herself," he added, straight-faced.

"How helpful you're going to be, Mr. Valentino," Aunt Maddie said gratefully. "I'm so glad you hired him, Worth."

"I can manage on my own. Truly," Melanie said, rising wearily from her chair.

Her father waved her back into her seat. "I won't hear

of it, pet. You stay put until Mr. Valentine can assist you. He's younger and stronger than the rest of us. Much safer."

Melanie sank back down, her eyes fixed on Peter's throat as she made a strangling gesture with her hands. He blithely ignored her and slung Brown over his shoulder so efficiently that the man didn't even awaken. Her father marched behind them to direct Peter to the butler's quarters.

Aunt Maddie watched their departure, then began to rave about the opera. Melanie managed to nod in the correct places, which was all the participation her aunt usually required in a conversation. Minutes later, Peter and her father reappeared. The younger man walked directly to her chair and offered his arm. "Come along," he instructed.

For one mad moment Melanie thought of making a scene, but in the Carroway household, even a wild-eyed protest didn't get the least bit of attention, a fact she'd learned by the time she reached the ripe old age of three. And their inherent capriciousness, of course, made her relatives totally oblivious to rational appeals. It was far easier just to flow with the currents of whatever whimsy gripped her family at the moment, no matter how odd it might seem to the rest of the world.

"I do hope you'll be all moved in by the weekend, Mr. Valentino," Aunt Maddie said gaily. "I always hold séances on Saturday nights, and if the spirits are kind, perhaps you can meet Harold—the first one, that is."

"Wouldn't miss it for the world, madam," Peter answered earnestly.

"You're only encouraging her," Melanie whispered.

Peter glanced at McNurty, who was nuzzling Aunt Maddie's ankle. "Hmmm . . . I think she already has all the encouragement she needs," he returned in a low voice.

He hooked an arm through hers, tugging her so close that her breast pressed against his rib cage. If she had thought for a moment that she could ignore his physical appeal, she knew differently now. A tingling flush flowed through her body as they swept from the room amid a flurry of hope-you-feel-betters and thank-yous.

Once they reached the curved staircase, Melanie attempted to pull free of Peter, but he kept a firm grasp on her. "Calm down," he cautioned. "Migraines are nothing to fool around with."

"I don't have a migraine," she informed him. "I don't even have a headache. I'm simply sick of being manipulated."

Peter continued to propel her up the stairs. "Your family's charming," he said.

"I adore them, but even to a perverse intellect such as yours, they must appear odd."

He shook his head, and the glossy waves of his blond hair sparkled in the iridescent light of the Waterford chandelier. An almost irresistible urge to reach up and touch his hair seized Melanie. She bit her lip, concentrating on putting one foot in front of the other. "Actually, Mel, they're the sanest bunch I've been around in a while," he went on. "My own family isn't exactly ordinary."

"That's easy to guess," Melanie countered, wondering how, short of shoving him down the stairs, she could remove her breast from his side. She couldn't stand much more physical intimacy with Peter. He was the most disconcerting male she'd ever known. Not that she had known all that many. Her family's enormous wealth and fine strain of madness, along with her own cautious reserve, had quickly discouraged even the most determined.

"Hmmm . . ." Peter purred, once more ignoring her sarcasm. "You have the softest curves, Mel."

"I am perfectly capable of walking by myself. Please let me go!"

He gasped aloud. "What? And offend your father? Cause that fine gentleman to think I'd shirked my duty? Disappoint your dear aunt? Be derelict—"

"Enough! Be quiet and get this over with. I just want to go to bed."

"Precisely what I'm attempting to help you do, my love," Peter explained, laughing.

They reached the third floor. "We're here," Melanie informed him, gesturing toward a double door with lead crystal knobs.

"Looks like a suite, not a room," Peter mused. "Better show me the inside so I can memorize the layout—for security reasons, naturally."

"Absolutely not."

"If not tonight, then in the clear light of day," Peter said authoritatively.

"No."

"Yes."

"I'm going to bed. Good night."

Peter's hand slid swiftly to the small of her back, pressing her into the hard length of his body. Her knees buckled slightly as she felt the thrust of his thighs against hers. "Why are you fighting me, Mel?" he demanded. "Don't you believe in karma? I felt it the minute you walked into the library."

In the dim light of the hall, his eyes were smoky, depthless. His hair seemed to be a tumble of silver and gold, falling in waves that skimmed the tops of his ears. He'd let the back grow low on the nape of his neck. The strands were thick and lustrous. He had very touchable hair, indeed.

With effort, she tore her eyes from him. "Because—because . . ." She was terribly tired, and confused, and her explanation failed to materialize.

Peter's free hand cupped her chin, forcing her to meet his gaze. For the first time, she noticed an interesting indentation at one corner of his mouth. Was it natural or a scar? In any case, it was very attractive, lending even more sensuality to a face that already had more than its fair share.

"This is all going to work out, Mel," Peter promised. "You'll see."

She shook her head sadly, knowing he was referring to more than the business agreement with her father. "N-no, it can't, Peter."

"Because of Harris?" he demanded gruffly.

"Not just him, although I've been seeing him off and on for years. He makes a decent escort, and he's reliable, mature, someone with whom I feel comfortable."

"Is that all you expect a man to be, Mel?" he asked in disbelief. "A decent escort?"

The phrase sounded ridiculous when he stressed the words in his husky slur. "You know what I mean," she said uneasily.

"No, I don't know what you mean." He pulled her onto her tiptoes so that their mouths were barely brushing. Just before he kissed her, he said, "But I do know what *I* mean. Believe it."

Chapter

3

THE NEXT DAY Melanie stayed in her room to paint, allowing only Cora inside with trays of food and drink. Despite the thick doors, Melanie still heard Peter's rich voice from time to time in the hallway. Apparently he was moving into what the family called the Tropical Paradise Room, only three doors down.

She was working with watercolors, attempting to finish a series of small landscapes she'd begun in Europe. Since it was necessary to paint some of them from rough sketches and memory, she needed the full power of her concentration. But every time she experienced the physical sensation Peter's voice created in her, she had to take a deep, calming breath.

"Damn him, anyway!" she swore repeatedly. Few things could distract her when she was painting. Art provided her with a lifeline to sanity, a healthy means of escape from the eccentricities of the other members of the household. Now that her marriage was over, she was determined to get together a portfolio to present to an exclusive gallery in Fort Worth. She desperately wanted to prove that she could be productive, perhaps even become an artist of some note. Over the years, her art professors had encouraged her to display her work, but she'd soon discovered the galleries weren't so much interested in her paintings as in any financial backing her wealthy family might provide them. After that, she'd refused to participate.

Recently, though, she'd heard about a certain small gallery downtown that was reputed to be exceptionally well financed and which exhibited only the finest art. A showing there would mean her paintings could truly stand on their own merit. That was important to her. She was eager to be accepted because of her talent, not just because she was a member of the fabulously wealthy but nutty Carroway tribe.

Toward the end of the afternoon, Melanie put away her brushes and curled up in the window seat to stare out the gabled windows at the rolling acreage of the estate. A rich carpet of autumn leaves covered the usually carefully tended grass. The caretaker had offered to rake them up, but her father told him not to bother. He enjoyed their color, and as an artist Melanie had to agree with him.

Rising, she walked into the adjoining bathroom to soak in the sunken tub. Often she did her best thinking while lying in warm, rose-scented bubbles, but today she just got waterlogged. She was no closer to putting her attraction to Peter Valentine out of her mind than she had been last night.

She supposed a therapist would tell her that people are often attracted to the opposite of what's good for them. Certainly the last thing she needed in her life right now was a madcap burglar. No doubt, he was temporarily enthralled by what he perceived to be a household straight out of a charming screwball comedy, which made him nearly as zany as her family. Although she loved her father and aunt, she felt they were somewhat responsible for her lack of confidence in herself.

Most people found it difficult to take her seriously once they learned her aunt conducted séances, the butler was a snobbish drunk, and her father presided over the crazy kingdom with a tolerant eye. Then, of course, there was McNurty. Once his role in the family was explained to outsiders, Melanie's last hope for a normal relationship was destroyed. Oh, a few had been fleetingly fascinated by the goings-on, but they had eventually succumbed to the desire for normalcy.

She couldn't cope very well with her family, particularly since she'd returned from Europe with her uncertain confidence severely shaken by her failed marriage. Yet, because she loved her father and aunt with a fierce devotion, she tended to be extremely cautious in forming new relationships.

Peter Valentine was the first man who'd entered the household, simply accepted things as they were, and brazenly launched into a full-scale attack on her wary senses. In a way, she admired him for that, but she suspected that allowing Peter to sweep her off her feet would be like signing up for chronic heartache.

She would never in a million years believe that Peter could fall in love with her. Certainly, he was fascinated by her and her strange companions, but soon he'd be disillusioned. No romantic interlude in the world was worth that kind of pain. In a few weeks Peter would be out of her life and she could concentrate on her painting. That would have to be enough.

At six-thirty, Melanie joined her family in the library for cocktails. Peter was sitting on the French-style love seat in front of a walnut bookcase, his arm draped casually over the plump upholstered back. She was as struck by his overwhelming charisma as she had been the previous night, she admitted reluctantly to herself.

His bold gaze burned into her as he examined the clinging white jersey dress with its delicately embroidered neckline that plunged almost to the jeweled waistline. A complete departure from her usual conservative wardrobe, the dress swirled in voluptuous folds around her smooth legs, showing a generous amount of creamy skin. Since she was determined not to become seriously involved with Peter, she couldn't for the life of her remember why she'd chosen such a shocking outfit. She patted her primly upswept hair self-consciously.

"How lovely you look, Melanie," Aunt Maddie said. "You must wear that frock to the séance tomorrow night.

The spirits are always more receptive when one is dressed for the occasion." McNurty, who lay at her aunt's feet, gave an enthusiastic belch.

Her father put down his newspaper and came to kiss her cheek. "I was just about to come check on you, you've been shut up in your room so long. Are you suffering from a headache, Melanie? If so, I'll call Dr. Dobbs and—"

"No, Father. I'm fine. Really," she assured him, remembering that a visit from the family physician was like spending an hour in Frankenstein's laboratory. The man's mental meanderings were in perfect harmony with the thought patterns of the other Carroways, however. Her relatives actually seemed to understand his free-flow logic. "I've been painting today, Father. That's why I cloistered myself in my room. There's so much I want to finish to get ready for—"

"Darling, you mustn't strain your eyes. That's one reason you suffer so from those damnable headaches."

Melanie sighed. Although she had tried a hundred times or so to convey to her father how much her painting meant to her, Worth Carroway took little note of anything outside of his own somewhat bizarre field of interest and, in a masterpiece of illogic, declared all artists to be half crazy.

Peter rose, gesturing for Melanie's father to be seated again, took her arm, and led her to the seat beside him. "You look wonderful," he whispered. "I've missed you today."

In spite of her resolve not to encourage him, Melanie found herself thinking he was the one who looked wonderful. He wore a three-piece navy blue suit, an immaculate pale blue silk shirt, and a classic foulard tie in muted blue, crimson, and off-white. "You look quite respectable yourself," she murmured.

Brown tottered precariously toward them and thrust a wavering tray of drinks under their noses. "Take one before I drop the confounded thing," he urged.

They complied immediately. Brown staggered off to the bar, slammed the tray down, and poured himself a whiskey—not his first, obviously. She stole an embarrassed glance at Peter, but his eyes were riveted on her décolletage. "You're breathtaking, Mel," he said softly. "Absolute perfection. You should always wear low-cut dresses to show off your creamy, well-shaped—"

"Please," she begged. "You're making me uncomfortable." Deliberately she didn't mention that she was also delighted by his lavish compliments.

He grinned. "Nobody's paying any attention to us, if that's what concerns you, Mel. See?"

It was true. Her father was immersed in the newspaper, and her aunt was playing checkers by herself. McNurty was asleep with his nose in his empty bourbon-and-water bowl. Brown, of course, wouldn't have noticed if Peter had thrown her onto the floor and ravaged her beneath the Louis XV escritoire. "Your behavior is hardly proper," she retorted priggishly.

"For an employee, you mean? Laying it on a bit thick, aren't you, Mel? Snobbism isn't your style; we both know that." Peter's arm still rested on the back of the love seat, but his hand slid down to caress her bare arm, setting off sparks of electricity.

The doorbell chimed. Peter continued to trail his fingers in fiery paths along Melanie's arm. When she moved slightly away, his hand simply followed.

"Doorbell," Aunt Maddie reminded everyone absently. Worth Carroway glanced expectantly at Brown, who reluctantly put down his glass.

"Want me to get that?" he demanded churlishly.

"If you don't mind."

The butler lurched out of the library and stumbled down the hall. Seconds later, he stood stiffly on the threshold and loudly announced, "Mishter Harrish Mortimer."

Melanie jumped to her feet and stepped away from the love seat. The last thing she wanted was for Harris to find Peter caressing her. He'd think the worst, and she wanted to keep his respect, if possible. Of all the men she knew, he'd been the most loyal.

Smoking a pipe and looking rather distinguished in a navy blue dinner jacket, Harris Mortimer strode into the room. "Good evening, everyone."

Worth Carroway nodded, and Aunt Maddie inclined her head slightly. McNurty let out a low, menacing growl.

Harris shot the dog a contemptuous look as he kissed Melanie's cheek. Peter was instantly at her side. "How did you get past the gate?" he demanded. "Your name isn't on the approved-entry list."

Harris frowned, then quickly remembered his manners. "Melanie gave me the code not long ago. I'm sorry, I don't believe we've met." He extended his hand.

Peter seized it so firmly that Harris winced. "I'm Peter Valentine."

"Peter's our new security analyst, Harris," Melanie hastily explained. "He's going to upgrade our entire system."

"And I'll be personal bodyguard to both of these lovely ladies," Peter added firmly.

Harris's eyebrows rose. "I see." His pale blue gaze took in the other man's powerfully muscled shoulders and intimidating stance. "Well, he looks as if he could do the job all right," he said to no one in particular. He turned his attention back to Melanie. "When did all of this come about?"

Before Melanie could steer Harris away, Peter volunteered an answer. "I began work last night," he explained. "Mr. Carroway hired me."

"Naturally," Harris answered knowingly, giving Melanie a sympathetic look. "I shouldn't be surprised, I suppose. There's always something unusual going on in this household."

Peter's jaw hardened. "Harris, I'm glad you dropped by. Saves me a trip into town. I need to have you answer some questions so you can be cleared."

"Cleared?" Harris echoed incredulously. "What on earth—?"

Melanie was furious. "Peter, this is totally unnecessary. I've known Harris for many years. He's my guest, and I won't have him subjected to some silly interrogation!"

"It'll just take a few minutes, Harris, old boy," Peter assured him in what to Melanie sounded suspiciously like a very good imitation of Harris himself. "Mr. Carroway agrees with me that everyone outside the immediate household should be screened so that I can revise the approved-entry list. Right, sir?" he shouted across the long room.

Worth Carroway looked up distractedly from his paper. "Quite right, Mr. Valentine," he mumbled vaguely, returning to his reading.

Harris ran a hand through his prematurely graying hair. "Melanie?" he appealed.

"Now, now, Harris, let's not make a mountain out of a molehill," Peter chastised. "We're screening everyone, even the delivery people. Doesn't that make you feel better?"

Before Harris could answer, Peter propelled him to a Regency gaming table in the corner farthest from Aunt Maddie, pushed him into a chair, and whipped a notepad and pen out of his pocket. Melanie rushed to join them. "Peter," she said between clenched teeth, "I'm warning you—"

He smiled ingenuously. "About what, Mel? Does Mr. Mortimer have some deep, dark secrets? Is he not all that he appears to be—a well-mannered, Harvard-educated, works-in-the-family-business type?"

"How did you know all that?" Harris demanded.

Melanie closed her eyes for a second. Harris Mortimer was no match for Peter Valentine. "He's guessing, Harris," she said, angry at both men. Peter was trying to make Harris look like a dunce. She sat down between the two men and listened resignedly as Peter proceeded to make Harris into an even bigger fool.

"Age?" Peter barked.

"Uh, thirty-six."

"Height?"

"Five-nine."

"Hmmm . . . I would have guessed you to be shorter. And you're what, maybe ten pounds overweight?"

"Well, I hardly think . . . well, maybe five."

"I'll put down eight as a compromise. What is your source of income, Mr. Mortimer?"

Harris puffed vigorously on his pipe, then answered stiffly, "Our family business, Mortimer Oil. No doubt you've heard of it."

"Ah, it does ring a faint bell. Of course, it's not as catchy as Sunoco or Standard, is it?"

Melanie sank slowly back in her chair as Peter continued to ask questions, dutifully jotting down the answers in a hand that resembled Sanskrit. At first Harris appeared only mildly irritated by Peter's brashness, but halfway through the interrogation, he grew obviously angrier, assuming the manner of a king being questioned by a peasant. By the end he was harrumphing frequently.

"Dinner is served!" Brown bellowed as the clock struck eight. Harris stood up so hastily, that he nearly knocked over the table.

"Wait!" Peter ordered. "One more thing before I can release you." He arched a brow and fixed Harris with a deadpan stare. "Do you like anchovies on pizza?"

"Good Lord! Is that what's being served for dinner?" Harris asked in disbelief.

Melanie's shoulders sagged. "Certainly not. And you don't have to respond to this—"

"Yes, he does," Peter corrected her. "It's very important."

"Well," Harris said uncertainly, "no, I don't like them. They're much too salty. I prefer formal dining to casual, actually."

Peter looked at Melanie triumphantly. "Such a shame."

Harris expelled a whoosh of tobacco-scented air in exasperation. "Look here, Mr. Valentine, your behavior has been unaccountably cryptic this evening, not to mention rude. I've indulged you until now only because I didn't want to upset Melanie any more than you already have. But I warn you that I've had quite enough and—"

"Surely, I don't understand you correctly, old sport." Peter's expression was pure innocence. "You're not threatening me, are you?"

"Peter—" Melanie began.

Harris made a silencing motion with his hand as he planted his feet slightly apart and thrust out his chest. "I feel compelled to advise you, Mr. Valentine, that I work out daily in my private gym." He cast a sidelong glance at Melanie, smiling boastfully. "I've worn out three punching bags in the last six months."

"Hmmm..." Peter replied thoughtfully. "Impressive. But if we're playing true confessions, I should inform you that I have a black belt in karate. I find the sport so much more civilized than boxing—not so much blood involved. Though, naturally, it has its drawbacks. Broken bones among them."

Harris nearly swallowed his Adam's apple. Melanie reached out to lay a reassuring hand on his arm, but he backed away. "My dear," he said shakily, "I hate to dash, but I really only stopped by to see how you were feeling. You had such a terrible headache when I called yesterday. At any rate, I do have business to attend to tonight. I'll call you soon." By the end of his apology, Harris's words were running together.

"Harris, please don't feel you have to go," Melanie pleaded. "I really would love for you to stay for dinner and—"

"Sorry, I don't think I could eat a thing." Harris nodded politely to Worth and Aunt Maddie as he rushed toward the front door, stopping only long enough to accept the hat and coat that the butler thrust at him.

"Cora didn't set a place for him anyway," Brown grumbled as he offered his arm to Aunt Maddie.

Dinner, as usual, was perfectly awful. The tomato aspic bore a suspicious resemblance to Jell-O, and the dessert defied identification. But Cook had been with them forever, and the family had grown used to her unorthodox concoctions. Only Melanie, who had been away until recently, had difficulty re-educating her palate.

Peter ate enormous portions, apparently finding absolutely nothing unusual about the meal. Nor did he question the fact that Brown, halfway through serving, sank down at the table and ate dinner with them instead of joining Cook and Cora in the kitchen. Peter even ignored the one-sided conversation Aunt Maddie held with McNurty, who lay at her feet eating from a Limoges plate. Melanie picked at her food, anticipating the moment she could get Peter alone and chastise him for his treatment of Harris.

She intercepted him on his way to the library to join the family for brandy. "Peter, I'd like to have a word with you in private," she said sweetly, aware her aunt and father could hear.

"By all means."

"If it's about Harris," her father said over his shoulder, "I've always considered him a bit of a wimp, Melanie, pet." With that, he, Aunt Maddie, McNurty, and Brown went into the library.

Peter's resounding chuckle echoed through the cavernous hallway. "My sentiments exactly."

"Come into the parlor," Melanie ordered

"I'd follow you to the ends of the earth," Peter replied cheerfully.

Ignoring him, she led the way into the elegantly furnished room and motioned for him to be seated in the sturdiest eighteenth-century chair.

"I suppose you're madder than hell," Peter commented matter-of-factly, sinking into the chair, one leg slung casually over the arm.

Melanie took a deep breath. "I hardly know where to begin. First, you insinuate yourself into this household. Then you take over our lives, and *then . . .*" She paused, trying to maintain what was left of her serenity. "And then you openly insult my most loyal friend."

"Suitor," Peter corrected, smiling meaningfully.

"That's an old-fashioned word." Her tone was icy. "Why don't you use 'lover' instead?"

"Because it's not accurate," he said, unruffled.

Melanie's brown eyes darkened, and she clasped her hands together at her waist. Her breasts rose and fell beneath the soft jersey dress as she struggled for control. "Of all the nerve! You don't know that."

Before she could move, Peter sprang from the chair and seized her shoulders in a firm though gentle grip. "I'm a trained observer, Mel, and I didn't get a hint of electricity. You know, the kind that emanates from people who have or want to have a sexual relationship. You see Harris as a way of passing the time—period." His eyes narrowed. "Mr. Prep School is reliable, respectable, and safe. I'll bet dating him is as exciting as sitting on Main Street watching the traffic lights change."

Melanie flushed. "Harris is dependable, mature, well-fixed, has a comparable background—"

Peter let out a snort of disgust, and a muscle in his jaw flexed. Would you honestly consider a serious relationship with a man who has the personality of a wall and the backbone of a snail?"

Peter's intense manner, and the feel of his fingers stroking the sensitive hollow below her collarbone, chased Melanie's anger away. "I can't defend Harris against someone like you," she said slowly, "but he's the kind of man I need right now. I've spent most of my life with unorthodox people, and although I love my family very much, I want a chance at a stable, ordered existence."

Peter slid a hand to her elbow and guided her to a camelback sofa in front of the inlaid-marble fireplace. He eased her onto a sumptuous velvet cushion and sat down next to her. "Tell me about your marriage," he said softly, encircling her nearly bare shoulders with his arm. The familiar electricity between them charged the air. How was it possible, Melanie wondered, that this man, who did not at all represent what she would have consciously chosen for herself, could make her go limp by simply touching her?

She forced her mind back into logical thought patterns. She was beginning to realize Peter's comments, which often seemed like non sequiturs, really weren't. "I waited a long time to marry," she answered bluntly. "My family made it difficult, as you can imagine. Many men were simply 'not up to snuff,' as my father would all too willingly inform them, or they were frightened off by the eccentricities of this household, or by what they considered a staggering amount of wealth. Occasionally, of course, there were those who were attracted only to my money."

Peter remained silent, his fingers tracing soothing configurations along her arm.

"So," she continued, "when I met Rip—"

"Rip?"

"Don't start," she warned, knowing full well the kind of malicious fun he could have with her former husband's name.

"I'll try to restrain myself," he promised solemnly. "Go on."

"Rip was dashing, exciting, witty, clever, handsome— and he made up the rules as he went along. I met him in Paris last fall, the first time I'd ever been abroad by myself." Melanie smiled bitterly. "The few other men I'd been involved with until then had been conservative in comparison. They lacked that special spark."

"So you threw caution to the wind and married Rip," Peter said.

"Yes." She sighed. "A month after we met. It was the biggest mistake I've ever made. You see, when you've been reared among assorted crazies, you react in one of two ways. Either you become like them, or you're determined to be the balancing, sensible force. I opted for the latter at an early age."

"Too bad," Peter murmured.

"It's just the way I was—am," she corrected. "I still don't know why I allowed myself to break my own code of behavior, but the fact remains that I did, only to regret it terribly before long. I suppose I thought that Rip, in spite of his quirky charm, was essentially a good, reliable person. By marrying him, I thought I could have the best of both worlds—that elusive thing called fun as well as dependability."

"The best of all combinations," Peter observed. "It's what everyone wants out of life." His expression was tender as he added softly, "You were looking for the right things, Mel, you just picked the wrong man. Don't keep punishing yourself for an understandably human error in judgment."

"I'll never make a mistake like that again," she said firmly, determined to convince Peter that a serious involvement with him was out of the question. "Being both fun and dependable is a contradiction in terms. One usually counteracts the other. As it turned out, Rip carefully researched my background, arranged to meet me, exuded charm all over me, and then systematically bilked me out of every dime he could get his hands on. His gambling and clothing bills were exorbitant, and the parties he gave were outlandishly expensive."

She paused, trembling slightly as she remembered the enormous sums of money Rip had kept demanding from her, the endless evenings when she'd stood in a corner while Rip and his jet set friends had ignored her or badgered her to loosen up. Their expensive illegal habits had disgusted her, as had their loose morals and their general aimlessness.

Peter's fingers traced her cheekbone, and suddenly she realized that his caress evoked more overwhelming emotion in her than her ex-husband ever had. "Go on," he encouraged gently.

"Finally, I caught on to Rip. I guess the turning point came one night in Monte Carlo when he lost two hundred thousand dollars in a little over an hour. He became very angry when I accused him of throwing money away, of preferring his flamboyant friends to me. He shouted that I wasn't any fun at all, always complaining, stingy . . . I told him quietly that I thought we should try living separately for a little while, that I wanted to get a job in an art gallery or a museum, work more on my own art."

"And?" Peter prodded.

Melanie shrugged. "He said he hated my art and I shouldn't take a job some other poor slob really needed, that I wasn't qualified to do anything of value anyway. His charm died rather quickly in the face of those devastating revelations. I left him, took back my maiden name, and returned to my family. Our marriage lasted less than six months."

Peter shook his head. "The guy was a total jerk, Mel. But everyone's entitled to make mistakes in love."

She nodded absently. "Rip was a pro. He dangled a wonderful carrot in front of my eyes, and I couldn't resist. He was just so much fun at first. Until he entered my life, my major source of excitement was the peculiar kind my family provides. And, believe me, after you live with that for a while, you don't find it all that thrilling." She sighed. "The divorce went through last month—finally. But even though the legalities are settled, my emotions aren't."

"Why did you come back here?" Peter asked quietly.

She made a small, helpless gesture. "I love my family, and this is a life I understand, even though I find it increasingly difficult to cope with my relatives. But I have an obligation to watch over them. Father has high blood pressure; Aunt Maddie's heart is weak. They're growing old. Also, I wanted to return to the States. Rip and I lived abroad the entire time we were married. My family met him only once—right before the wedding. Naturally, he was on his best behavior. Maybe if they'd been able to stick around longer than two days, they would have discovered what he was before I did."

"They left hurriedly?" Peter asked, puzzled.

"Yes. They didn't arrive until the day before the wedding because they kept missing their flight over. They just couldn't make it to the airport in time—forgot their luggage, their medication, whatever. Then, at the reception, Aunt Maddie and Father got into a terrible fight with the hotel people." Melanie bit her lip. "Here we all were in this elegant ballroom, and McNurty ran amok after drinking too much champagne. The damned dog ate most of the wedding cake, two linen tablecloths, several ounces of caviar, and part of a velvet drape. Father, Aunt, and McNurty were kicked out of the hotel."

Peter's amazement gave way to a burst of laughter.

Angrily, Melanie slid away from him. "I'm glad you think it's so funny, Peter! Just how would you have reacted if it'd been *your* wedding?" She fixed him with a savage glare. "I told Aunt Maddie and Father that McNurty was not invited, but they insisted on bringing him, even paid a healthy sum for the management to look the other way and allow him to have his own suite next to my aunt's! I nearly died when I saw all of them arrive."

Peter remained silent for a few seconds, then asked mischievously, "Was the original Harold McNurty a drunk?"

Melanie hurled an embroidered bolster at him, but Peter

blocked the hit with an agile thrust of his forearm. "Come on, Mel, I just want you to see the humor in the situation. McNurty, I admit, probably wasn't the world's classiest wedding guest, but that one embarrassing moment just isn't worth brooding over. You have to make the best of bad moments like that. What else can you do? Sink deeper into your shell? Become so uptight that you have headaches all the time? Deny your true feelings because you're afraid of making another mistake?"

"Yes, to all of the above questions," she answered tensely. "My family always overprotected me when I was younger, so when I grew up, I had very little idea of how to cope with life. My relatives meant well. They still do. But their view of life is drastically skewed. Father honestly believes that everyone who isn't on welfare is as rich as we are. He thinks some people drive Chevies because they prefer them to Rolls-Royces. And believe it or not, he thinks some women wear rhinestones because diamonds are an endangered species! Aunt Maddie sees things from the same tilted perspective. And Brown is the true snob in this household; he looks down on anyone who isn't a *butler*. Lord, Peter, they're all impossible!"

He regarded her seriously for a moment. "Mel, there's a halfway point between your family's eccentricity and your stubborn adherence to convention. But if you have to lean in one direction or the other, you'd be better off slanting your views toward theirs. At least, they enjoy life."

She looked away from him, clenching her teeth.

Peter rose from the sofa and went to stand against the mantel in a characteristic pose, one elbow propped on the smooth marble surface, the thumb of his other hand hooked in his belt. "Your family's delightful, Mel. True, they have a different way of going about things. But they're happy with themselves and unusually perceptive in their own cloudy way."

"That's a very romantic appraisal, Peter. Unfortunately, it has nothing whatsoever to do with reality."

"What happened to your mother?" Peter asked, ignoring her put-down.

Melanie shrugged. "She left when I was ten. Ran off with a musician Father had hired for a party. We never heard from her again. The stuff of which soap operas are made. Mother was a very irresponsible person."

"And your father's been pretty much of a recluse ever since," Peter guessed.

"Exactly," she admitted, surprised by his keen perception. "Father never again bothered to take an active part in his business interests. Our family attorney handles all of that now. Everything around here sort of ground to a halt— the glamorous parties, the family vacations, the constant stream of people in and out of the house. I don't think Father consciously withdrew from real life. He simply joined my aunt in the fantasy world she has always lived in. The two of them seem to encourage each other's eccentricities. They rarely go anywhere, and, most of their friends have dropped out of their lives."

Peter looked thoughtful. "So, over the years charmingly different became endearingly eccentric."

Melanie heard the despair in her own voice as she spoke. "Not everyone finds their peculiarities endearing, I'm afraid. I had a lonely childhood. I knew my peers wouldn't understand about my family. They were all from normal households. When I was eleven, Father gave me a birthday party. He hired an entire circus, not just a clown. My schoolmates and their parents were flabbergasted. They thought my family was showing off." Her eyes brightened. "I couldn't explain that it never occurred to Father that hiring a three-ring circus was in bad taste. Having too much money is nearly as bad as not having enough, I think. The Carroway wealth has sheltered us from real life in many respects. Consequently, we often show poor judgment in matters other people have learned to deal with through trial and error."

"Including you?"

"Yes," she replied sadly.

"It's never too late to learn what you need to know to be happy, Mel," Peter argued. "You're going about your education in all the wrong ways, deliberately avoiding life's challenges—especially with regard to matters of the heart."

She stood with her hands clenched tightly at her sides. "That assumption is another prime example of how you overstep your bounds, Peter. I am choosing a life for myself, not allowing life to choose it for me. There's a big difference. I haven't given up, either. In fact, I'm determined to lead a normal life, preferably near my family so I can keep an eye on them."

"And so," Peter said in razor-sharp tones, "Mr. Harris Milquetoast Mortimer re-enters the picture. No doubt he's been hanging around for years, waiting for you to seriously cast those big brown eyes his way. And hasn't he been patient? He waited while you went to school and then went to school some more. Your aunt told me you have two graduate degrees. Then Mr. Mortimer even had the good breeding to forgive you your impetuous, in-questionable-taste marriage. Well, it's all perfect, Mel. A safe, predictable life. But, oh, so boring."

Melanie jabbed a trembling finger in his direction. "Don't make the mistake of analyzing me again, Peter. You don't know anything about me—not really. Not the part of me that counts." She stepped toward him, her voice shaking. "Security is your business, but you don't know a damned thing about protecting the human heart. So stop pontificating, tighten our security, and get out of our lives as quickly as possible."

Peter moved so swiftly that she didn't realize what he was doing until he caught her in his arms. Tipping her chin up, he said firmly, "I'm here to stay, Mel. What I'm doing interests your father. He's excited about the technology of it, understands how important it is to have decent security. I think he even likes me. We had some interesting conversations today, and I'll bet we can learn a lot from each other. Don't try to take that opportunity away from your father, not if you truly care about him."

"I—I won't," she said breathlessly. Summoning her iron-clad resolve, she added firmly, "But don't think your relationship with Father gives you the right to take personal liberties with me, or to find fault with my choices. You're here to do a job, and if that amuses my father, fine. Just don't practice your idea of security on *me*."

"I assume, once again, you're not just talking about locks, bolts, and electronic gadgetry," Peter said caustically.

"Right."

The fingers on her chin tightened slightly.

"I told you, Peter," she insisted, "I want to start leading as normal an existence as possible, but I don't want to be amused by you."

"You're afraid," he accused harshly.

She lowered her lashes, unable to meet his penetrating gaze. "Yes. And uninterested," she shot back cruelly.

"Hasn't anyone ever told you, Mel, that you can't possibly win if you never take a chance?" Peter's tone was scornful.

"I did take a chance—once—and it was a big mistake. I'm not up to what you call excitement. I guess I'm not cut out for life in the fast lane." Meeting Peter's eyes, Melanie imagined the pain this man could cause her when he grew tired of trying to make her into someone she wasn't, and delivered the final blow. "I know what I want, what I need. You don't begin to fit the bill, Peter."

His eyes caressed her face in a fluid sweep. He bent still closer, and his lips covered hers. The kiss began as the others had, firmly yet gently. But this time his tongue invaded her mouth, flicking over her teeth, then stroking the soft tissues, tantalizingly, sensuously.

Melanie lifted one hand in the feeble beginning of a protest, then let it flutter helplessly as he drew her against his hard chest. She felt her nipples brush against the soft fabric of her dress and a feverish burning sensation spread throughout her body. And then Peter simply walked away, leaving her with her arms hanging limply at her sides, a telltale flush coloring her high cheekbones, and a desperate ache just below her heart.

He paused at the door, and without turning around, said grimly, "Ask Harris to kiss you like that the next time he drops by. And then tell me honestly if he makes you feel the same way I do."

Chapter

4

MELANIE CHECKED HER reflection in the mirror again, gently probing her temples, peering closely at the area under her eyes. Amazing. There was no incipient throb. No dark circles. After spending a restless, mostly sleepless night, she'd expected at least the first signs of a headache, but there were none. In fact, she felt perfectly fine, except for a vague sense of . . . what was it exactly? Longing. That was the word.

Damn Peter Valentine anyway! His intimate, brash way of making his point last night had disturbed her more than she would ever admit to him. She'd never known anyone with such colossal nerve, such a lack of concern for propriety, such a preoccupation with sex. He was absolutely depraved! He ought to be put away.

A smile tugged at the corners of her mouth at a mental image of Peter in a padded cell. A few months of being locked up would teach him a lesson. Unless, of course, his keeper happened to be a susceptible female. In that case, it was all too easy to imagine who would end up keeping whom. Some women, no doubt, found Peter Valentine's sexual innuendoes arousing, his charm devastating . . .

And she, unfortunately, was one of them. The smile transformed itself into a frown. What was the matter with

her? He was just another version of Rip, although she suspected Peter wasn't after her money, only her heart. But,
like her ex-husband, who had left when he'd taken all he
could get, Peter would discard her like an old shoe after
he'd met the challenge of breaking down her reserve. And
she'd be left with the last vestiges of her self-respect in
tatters, a poor little rich girl.

Angrily Melanie turned away from the dressing table
mirror, jerked a painter's smock out of the closet, and went
to stand in front of her easel. A half-finished Alpine land-
scape awaited the addition of a few realistic details. She
stared at its orderly pastel serenity for a few minutes, then
put it to one side. Selecting a primed canvas, she squeezed
a circle of scarlet oil on her palette and began to paint,
allowing her imagination to dictate her strokes.

With no specific intention in mind, no image imprinted
on her retina, she worked hesitantly, uncertain as to what
she was creating. Her best work had always been highly
representative of something or someone she'd seen in a
photograph or real life. Rarely had she allowed herself to
indulge her emotions by experimenting with abstract expres-
sionism. But today she felt adventurous. An hour went by.
She added cobalt blue to the voluptuous swirls of scarlet.
Another hour passed. The canvas now glowed with strokes
of four colors. Teal blue and bright yellow slashes swooped
vividly among the scarlet and cobalt blue swirls. The aimless
brush strokes of a child, Melanie thought ruefully.

She laid down her brushes and removed her smock. Maybe
if she went downstairs and had a cup of tea, her sudden
need to paint in the nonobjective style would disappear. She
suddenly wanted to get back to landscapes, a familiar genre
she knew was suited to her talent, and in which she felt
comfortable and . . . safe. Free-form art made her nervous.

In the kitchen she found Aunt Maddie supervising the
preparation of McNurty's midmorning breakfast. The dog
had taken to sleeping in and rarely ate before ten-thirty. Her
aunt, of course, indulged him in his lazy habits.

"Good morning, darling," Aunt Maddie said brightly,
placing a porcelain bowl on the floor. "McNurty wanted

coddled eggs this morning, so Cook went to a great deal of trouble to fix them." She smiled happily as she watched the dog eat noisily. "What have you been doing, dear?" she added absently, bending over to add more salt to McNurty's eggs.

Melanie finished preparing a cup of tea and joined her aunt at the table. "I've been painting."

"Ah, how nice. Do you think that sometime soon you can get started on the portrait of McNurty and me? I don't want to pressure you, darling, but you know how important it is to capture the true essence of people at the right time. My charts indicate that all of the proper astrological signs will be moving into place before long."

"Aunt, I don't want to disappoint you, but I do have some work of my own to finish, you know, and—"

"I'd like a crimson background this time," Aunt Maddie said wistfully. "That would blend in nicely with the other portraits in the McNurty gallery in the east wing, don't you think?"

"Yes, I suppose so."

Her aunt beamed. "A good sense of color runs in the family." Sighing, she added, "I only wish you'd been able to paint the first two McNurtys. It was such a nuisance having to hire an artist to come to the house. Outsiders just don't understand what I have in mind. Now, I know it's not your fault that you weren't born when Harold was reincarnated the first time, and that you were too young during the second one's—"

"Aunt," Melanie interrupted gently, "we'll begin the portrait as soon as possible. Next week we'll set a definite time. Will that be all right?"

"Oh, perfect, darling." Her aunt clapped her hands together in delight. "I'll have Brown groom McNurty. I just hope he doesn't clip him too short this time. Harold had a head full of lovely hair, and to do the portrait justice—"

"I'll ask Brown to be more careful," Melanie assured her aunt.

"Thank you, dear. I'd appreciate it. I can't communicate with Brown as well as I once could." Aunt Maddie shook her head sadly. "Poor man. He's in constant pain, so I suppose he has difficulty concentrating."

"Brown takes too much medicine, Aunt," Melanie said firmly.

"Now, now, we are in no position to judge him, Melanie—" A loud pounding from the basement interrupted her. Melanie jumped, and McNurty spewed coddled eggs all over the tiled floor. "Goodness! I hope Mr. Valentino and Jennifer are all right down there," Aunt Maddie said, peering distractedly toward the open basement door.

"Jennifer?" Melanie asked in surprise. "Peter's in the basement? With a *woman?*"

Her aunt nodded absently, stroking McNurty's head. "Yes, I saw him less than an hour ago. He said he was going down to coax Jennifer into behaving."

"Jennifer who?" Melanie asked, aware her voice had risen.

"I have no idea, darling. I didn't meet the young woman."

Melanie took a deep breath. Aunt Maddie's revelation proved what she'd always suspected about Peter. His kisses were indiscriminate, therefore meaningless. He was as frivolous as Rip had been. She bit her lip, remembering the countless times she'd caught her ex-husband kissing and fondling other women. He'd tried to dismiss his infidelities by accusing her of being a prude. Lord, how his cavalier attitude toward commitment had hurt her. The pain was still there, just below the cool exterior she tried so hard to maintain. And now Peter had reopened that old wound. Damn him! For some reason her heart felt even heavier now than it had during Rip's dalliances.

But that wasn't why she was going to confront him, she assured herself as she marched downstairs. Absolutely not. She merely intended to inform Peter he was sadly mistaken if he thought he could use his job as a front for pursuing sexual flirtations! He was taking advantage of her father's faith in his so-called professionalism, and it was her duty to set Peter straight immediately!

The basement consisted of a series of winding tunnels that jutted out in four directions from a main room. Her father always said the passages would make useful hiding places if Forth Worth were under attack. Melanie stood in the center of the room, trying to decide which way to go.

The not-too-distant sound of Peter's raised voice made the decision for her. She followed it, stalking down the dimly lit east tunnel, which led to the wine cellar. She passed several closed doors and was ready to jerk open the one to the wine cellar when she heard Peter's voice again, low, soothing, and huskily seductive, coming from a partly open door next to the wine cellar. So, he'd stopped trying to intimidate this Jennifer person and was now using his come-hither tones to get what he wanted. How disgusting!

Melanie threw the door wide open. Peter was bent over a long table. Parts of what looked like a computer were spread out in front of him. He turned in surprise as she stomped forward. "All right, where is she?" Melanie demanded, scanning the room. "Behind those cartons?" She gestured at a pile of boxes in the far corner. "Or did you stuff her in that closet over there?" Her trembling finger indicated a closed door.

Peter straightened slowly, his expression perplexed but not overly concerned. "Have you lost something, Mel?"

"No, but you certainly have. Your job, for one thing," she answered between clenched teeth.

"Oh?" Peter smiled. "I don't think so. Your father's the only one who can fire me."

"And he will once he's heard about this latest—" Melanie paused, trying to get her breath. "Depravity!" she exclaimed."

"Depravity?" Peter echoed. "I'm dying to find out what you're accusing me of this time, Mel."

She marched over to the cartons, shoving them aside. Nothing. Jennifer had to be hiding in the closet. She walked deliberately toward it, turned to give Peter a triumphant look, and pulled the door open. She had just enough time to see that no one was in there before a pile of precariously stacked boxes of clothing tumbled down on her head.

She was trying to wriggle free of an ostrich feather boa that had snaked around her neck and a velvet cape, whose hook and eye were ensnared in her hair, when Peter began to laugh. How infuriating! She tore at the boa, which slithered to the floor, and fumbled with the cape, finally managing to disentangle it from her hair and throw it into the heap at her feet. He auburn hair hung in disarray about her flushed cheeks.

"What a mess you've made, Mel," Peter observed wryly.

Melanie waded through the scattered clothing, kicking it aside as she strode determinedly toward Peter. "Where is she?" she asked tightly.

Peter placed both hands on her shoulders. "Mel, I'm not a mind reader. Tell me what you're talking about." One hand cupped her trembling chin, forcing her to look into his eyes. His gaze flickered sympathetically as he observed her distress.

She took a deep breath. Peter's touch was as upsetting as her anger. Maybe more so. She bent her head, fighting for control, then slowly lifted her eyes to his again. "Where's Jennifer?" she asked frostily.

He smiled. "Jennifer? You mean the most exasperating, complicated, wonderful-when-she's-obliging—"

Melanie jerked away from him. "Stop it! I don't want to hear this, Peter. It's in extremely bad taste."

"I'm sorry, but that's really how I think of her. I'm afraid I'm honest to a fault when it comes to the inner workings of—"

"Inner workings?" Melanie cried. "Oh, you're horrible. You talk about Jennifer as if she were a machine, something put on this earth entirely for your convenience."

A muscle in his jaw began to twitch; then he doubled over in a fresh outburst of laughter.

Melanie stared at him. Where on earth did Peter find the nerve to laugh so hard when he'd broken every rule of professional behavior on only his second day on the job?

Without a word he grabbed her hand and led her to the table that was littered with delicate electronic components. He pointed to a large box, with funny-looking wires dangling over the flaps. Silently she read aloud the bold-faced print on the side of the box: "Maker of the world's finest electronic instruments. Jennifer Corporation. New York, New York."

Was there a hole big enough for her to disappear into? Could she, by wishing hard enough, create a natural disaster that would swallow up both Peter and her? Might the roof fall in as a momentary diversion? A few more seconds passed before she was able to square her shoulders and force herself to raise her eyes to Peter, who was regarding her with what almost looked like tenderness. She spread her hands helplessly. "Jennifer, I gather, is a computer," she murmured.

Peter smiled. "Sort of. It's the control center for the whole surveillance system." He moved forward and took her in his arms. His lips brushed her flaming cheek and he said huskily, "I like the idea of your being jealous, Mel. It's very flattering. And besides, it gives me hope that you might really be starting to care."

She intended to mumble a protest first, then explain how the perfectly understandable mistake had occurred, and then assure him that she was not jealous. She'd simply felt she needed to protect her father's interests. But Peter's hand slid to the base of her spine, and his mouth rained fiery kisses along her neck. It was distracting, to say the least. But welcome, she admitted. As welcome and refreshing as the restraint he showed by not pointing out what a fool she'd made of herself. He lifted his head to cover her lips with his own. How was it possible that a man's kiss could say so much, could be at once forgiving, conciliatory, and unbelievably arousing?

When at last he withdrew his lips from hers, Melanie realized her cheeks were no longer crimson from embarrassment but from Peter's sensual reassurances. "I'm terribly sorry for my behavior," she apologized in a low voice. "I usually don't act so hastily. You see, Aunt Maddie told me you were down here trying to coax someone named Jennifer into behaving, and then I heard you talking to what I assumed was a woman. I thought you had—uh—brought a date to the house when you were supposed to be working."

Peter stroked the silky strands of her hair. "I'm afraid I

get a little carried away when I'm tailoring a security system to the individual needs of a client. If I can't get things right, I often get impatient and pound the table in sheer frustration. On the other hand, if things are going well, I murmur softly in encouragement."

"Like people who talk to their plants," Melanie concluded.

Peter grinned. "Yeah. Sort of."

They stood only inches apart as he continued to run his hand through her hair, brushing it back from her face. His touch was gentle, soothing, and absolutely mesmerizing. As her awareness became focused on the pleasing sensations he was arousing, her limbs grew heavy and her eyes drifted closed. How kind he was being to her. How charming. Just like Rip had been when she'd first known him . . .

She drew back suddenly, and Peter's hand fell away from her hair. "I've got to get back to my painting. I know you're busy, too. I'll see you later." She was nearly out the door of the storage room when Peter seized her shoulder and spun her about, pulling her to him and looking into her face for a long moment.

"Don't ever make the mistake of confusing me with your ex-husband, Mel, or assuming that I'll act the same way he did. Give me a fair chance to be me." His fingers fleetingly caressed her face before he released her.

Melanie mechanically made her way out the door and down the hallway, not stopping until she came to the main room of the basement. She stood very still then, lifting a trembling hand to where Peter had touched her cheek. Only then did she allow herself to wonder how he'd known what she was thinking.

Late that afternoon, Peter strode unannounced into Melanie's room. She whirled around on the stool in front of her easel, jerking off the glasses she wore for close work. "Haven't you ever heard of knocking?" she demanded crossly.

"Cat burglars don't knock, Mel. I long ago got out of the habit."

Melanie dropped the subject. Arguing with Peter was

like disagreeing with Aunt Maddie. One could never win. "Do you need something?" she asked.

He smiled disarmingly. "Lots of things. But for right now I'll settle for seeing some of your work."

"Why?"

"Because I'm interested." He walked over to examine the abstract painting on the easel. Melanie tried to block him by raising her arm, but he merely ducked under it and studied the bright slashes of color.

"This is very good, Mel," he finally said.

"Don't be silly. It's awful. I've just been experimenting."

"You should do it more often. I love the colors and the theme."

"Theme?" she echoed stupidly.

"Uh-huh. Can't you see the struggle going on in this work? The powerful emotion expressed?"

"No."

"Too bad. But you will eventually if you continue to allow your imagination as much freedom as your intellect."

Melanie sighed for about the fortieth time since her path had crossed Peter Valentine's. "I have some landscapes you might like to see," she offered, hoping to divert his attention from further analysis of what she considered an artistic failure.

She could have saved her breath. Peter was already carefully examining the stack of landscapes on the table next to the easel. "Very competent," he commented, flipping through them.

"Competent?"

"Hmmm . . . but this one is exceptional, Mel."

She peered nearsightedly at the canvas he held up. "Please give me that," she begged. "It's not very good, and it's intensely personal."

"It's wonderful," Peter said, ignoring her protest. "A self-portrait. If you're thinking of exhibiting anything, this one should be your first choice." He traced the curve of her cheek in the oil painting, the halo of her dark red hair, and finally the slight pout of her lower lip. "This is you, Mel— vulnerable, yet wary. Confused, but certain. This portrait expresses the full depths of your personality. You've captured your essence in a way no candid photo could ever hope to do."

"You sound like Aunt Maddie—talking about essence," Melanie said, flustered. Except for a couple of professors in graduate school, no one had ever shown such interest in her work before. "What makes you an expert on art anyway?"

His thickly lashed eyes met hers over the canvas. "I've been hired to protect some of the finest art in the world, Mel, and I've learned a lot along the way. Believe me when I say this portrait and the work on your easel are your best pieces."

Melanie turned away, pretending to sort through her brushes. She didn't know how to handle Peter Valentine, or what to make of him. One moment he made her so angry with his insensitive, brash comments. The next he was stirring up sensual feelings that threatened to overwhelm her. Then there was his offbeat humor, and the confusingly gentle side of him that understood and encouraged her as no one ever had. Not only was the man too complicated for her; he was much too unpredictable.

"You'd better get ready, Mel. It's late," Peter said, coming to stand behind her. His hands rested on her shoulders. She could feel the whisper of his breath on the back of her neck, smell the scent that was distinctively his. One hand lifted from her shoulder to brush aside her hair, and then his mouth trailed tiny kisses on the nape of her neck.

"Get ready?" she echoed faintly, swaying against his chest as if gravity were exercising an irresistible tug on her weightless body.

"Mmmm . . . it's after five. First dinner, then the séance."

She pulled away. "I'm not attending the séance, Peter. I haven't participated in years. My family's at their worst at those gatherings."

"I promised your aunt we'd both attend," he said firmly. "She'll be very hurt if you force me to tell her you don't want to come."

"I'll, I . . . have a headache," Melanie declared. "I always do before the séances."

"A very convenient excuse, isn't it, Mel? Well, don't bother talking yourself into a migraine tonight because I'll drag you along anyway." He smiled lackadaisically.

"You are the most insufferable—"

"See you at dinner, Mel," he returned breezily, striding toward the door. *"And* at the séance."

Melanie sat at the round, cloth-covered table in the parlor, her eyes darting nervously among the flickering shadows cast by candles on the mantel. Peter sat on one side of her, Worth Carroway on the other. Next to him was Brown, then McNurty in his own chair and finally Aunt Maddie reigning supreme over the Ouija board.

"First of all," Aunt Maddie said briskly, "we must be in the proper frame of mind to conjure up Harold's spirit. So, let us—"

"Don't forget about Jasmine," Brown interrupted querulously.

"Who's Jasmine?" Peter whispered to Melanie.

"His long-deceased parrot," she returned, thinking how Peter deserved everything he was going to get tonight.

"I won't, Brown," Aunt Maddie promised. "Please forgive me for my selfishness. I know you haven't been as fortunate as I with reincarnations."

Melanie leaned toward Peter. "He hasn't been as fortunate because my father has never been able to buy a parrot at the pet store and coax it to sit on the front step like the dogs," she whispered. "Father rings the bell, Aunt opens the door, and voilà! A fresh McNurty!"

In a low, horrified voice, Peter said, "Are you telling me that all of the McNurtys have been fakes?"

Oh, he was infuriating! She'd intended to make him uncomfortable for forcing her to attend this fiasco, and now he was baiting her. "Only the canine ones," she murmured acidly.

"Please clasp hands," Aunt Maddie requested.

Everyone complied. Peter seized the opportunity to caress Melanie's palm with tiny, featherlike swirls. She shivered as darts of icy heat shot up her arm. "Stop it," she demanded, more loudly than she'd intended.

"Is something wrong, Melanie?" her father asked.

Peter chuckled

"N-no. I'm sorry, Father."

"Let us begin," Aunt Maddie intoned passionately. For the next few minutes, Melanie endured her aunt's pleas to the spirit world and Peter's maddeningly sensual assault on her palm.

"Harold, can you hear me?" Aunt Maddie asked. "Do speak to us, darling." Her fingers rested lightly on the planchette. Slowly, the indicator began to move toward the *H* on the board.

"Amazing," Peter whispered.

It was more amazing that she was still sitting here, Melanie thought, one hand lovingly wrapped in her father's, the other sensuously captured in Peter's. And what the latter appendage was doing to her libido was most amazing of all. Until now she'd never fully understood the phrase "hot and bothered."

"I love you, Harold," Aunt Maddie said. "Just as I love everyone at this table, although of course not in *exactly* the same way. But they are very dear to me—even Mr. Valentino, who came to us only recently."

The planchette jumped rapidly to spell out the rest of Harold's name. "Ah, dearest, you *are* listening," Aunt Maddie cried excitedly. "Know, then, that we all care about you, that we are reassured by McNurty, your latest reincarnation here on earth." The dog howled enthusiastically. "Know that I appreciate the signs you have sent as proof that you are you, darling. All of the McNurtys have had your endearing traits, Harold. They cock their heads just the way you used to; they like the same foods; they like to sleep in late."

Peter released Melanie's hand and traced exciting whorls of electricity up her arm. Aunt Maddie spoke again, more fervently than before: "Love is the most powerful emotion of all, Harold. Feel the love in this room. Its force transcends the mistakes we make with each other, enables us to forgive what we don't understand—"

"Yes," Peter said, continuing his finger-light touch on

Melanie's bare arm, "love is alive and well in this household, misguided and misunderstood though it may sometimes be. The important thing is that love exists, and no one can doubt its power to make us into the very best we can be."

"Peter," Melanie began, astonished by his sincerity, even more disturbed by the unsettling emotions she was experiencing.

"Go ahead, Melanie dear," Worth Carroway murmured. "Tell us what's in your heart."

She couldn't very well say murder was in her heart. Anyway, to be perfectly honest, she was deeply affected by the close communion they were sharing. There was something about sitting together in a darkened room, holding hands and talking about love, that made her forget her embarrassment over the séances, despite her growing suspicion that Peter's presence was a major source of her newfound awareness. "I—I just want to say that I'm very happy to be here tonight . . . with all of you," she said softly.

"Bravo, darling!" her father cried enthusiastically. "And may I say how happy we are that you could join us this evening. We've missed you at our little gatherings."

"What about Jasmine?" Brown demanded, though not as gruffly as before.

"Oh, yes," Aunt Maddie said. "Now, spirits, if you would favor us with proof that Brown's dear departed parrot is among you . . ." The indicator swung abruptly to a *J*, next an *A*. Then a rush of wind tore at the velvet curtains in the room, and the candles went out. A noise that resembled squawking came from the front hall.

"Jasmine!" Brown cried excitedly, stumbling from the table toward the sound.

"Oh, my! An actual spiritual presence here among us!" Aunt Maddie gasped. McNurty barked loudly, and Worth Carroway cleared his throat ominously.

"Sit still!" Peter ordered, withdrawing his hand from Melanie's arm and disappearing into the darkness. Seconds later, Peter hit the master switch, and light flooded the room. He dashed in front of the family as they rushed into the hall. Brown had already managed to find his way from the darkened room and was glaring down at Harris Mortimer, who was sprawled out on the hallway floor with the heavy marble umbrella stand across his midriff. The front door stood wide open, and wind gusted through it.

"Harris!" Melanie cried, rushing to his side.

"Hmmph!" Brown muttered. "That's not Jasmine!" He stalked away in disgust.

"Oh, my!" Aunt Maddie said. "You really shouldn't interrupt a séance, Harris. The spirits will be most displeased."

"Indeed," Worth Carroway agreed as McNurty ambled over to sniff suspiciously at Harris, then backed away.

Harris started to sputter. Melanie turned frantically to Peter, who was standing casually at the edge of the gathering, apparently relaxed now that he knew no one was in any danger. "Could you please help me get this umbrella stand off Harris?" she pleaded.

He arched a brow, then lifted the stand as if it were made of papier-mâché. Setting it in its proper place, he hauled Harris up and kicked the door shut. "What in the hell do you mean by bursting in here and causing a disturbance?" he demanded icily.

The older man dusted off his clothes with one hand and massaged a rib with another. "I tripped in the dark, knocked into that confounded umbrella stand, or it knocked into me," he answered indignantly. "Don't any of you people believe in keeping lights on?"

"Not during séances," Aunt Maddie said firmly. "The spirits shed their own radiance." She took Worth Carroway's arm, and they went into the library, McNurty lumbering along behind them.

"Melanie, don't tell me you actually agreed to participate in such nonsense!" Harris said incredulously. "I thought you'd given up that drivel years ago."

"If only I'd finished installing the new security system," Peter returned coolly, "we wouldn't be listening to *your* drivel now. And I want to make it quite clear that Mel was enjoying the séance until you came crashing in."

"Peter, please," Melanie chastised him, absently massaging her temples.

"Look there! See what you've done by encouraging Melanie to go along with all of this nonsense!" Harris accused. "It's obvious she's suffering from a migraine!"

Peter's eyes settled on Melanie. "Do you have a headache?" he asked softly.

She gazed back at him, about to agree automatically with Harris when she suddenly realized that she *didn't* have a headache. In fact, she felt fine, not even overly agitated over the situation.

"No, I don't have a headache."

Peter rewarded her honesty with a dazzling smile, then glared at Harris. "The lady says she doesn't have a headache."

Harris looked skeptical. "Is that the truth, Melanie?"

"Yes," she said, watching Harris's face cloud in disappointment. Good heavens, were her migraines going to become a point of honor between Peter and Harris?

Peter registered the other man's expression and narrowed his eyes. "Too bad, isn't it, Harris, old sport? I mean, if Melanie's overcome her headaches, what daring thing might she do next? Boggles one's mind to think of the possibilities: She could start living her life as she wishes, fall in love with whom she chooses. Maybe even run away to join the circus!"

Harris turned crimson. "You are completely without redeeming qualities, Mr. Valentine. I'll be relieved when you're out of this household once and for all. You do nothing but encourage even more erratic behavior—the last thing this family needs!" He turned on his heel and left, slamming the door behind him.

Melanie was so confused that she didn't know exactly what she felt, except a growing sense of well-being. How strange. Outrageous things had been going on all evening, and yet she had remained relatively unruffled. A first for her. She started to speak, but before she could, Peter winked broadly, smiled, and said, "At least Harris went out with a bang instead of a whimper."

Chapter

5

MELANIE'S SENSE OF well-being all but disappeared three days after the séance. She still couldn't concentrate on the landscapes she wanted to finish. Of course, to be perfectly honest, she was having difficulty thinking about anything except Peter and his ever stronger physical effect on her. If he merely brushed her arm at dinner or "accidentally" bumped her hip when passing by, her spine turned to jelly. It was very disconcerting.

Worse, she knew beyond a shadow of a doubt that Peter was enjoying every minute of her discomfiture! Besides that, the man seemed to have eyes in the back of his head. Wherever she went, he turned up not long afterward. The way he tracked her every move was more than annoying—it was driving her crazy! Which must be why she found herself behaving totally out of character. Strange moods and impulses kept overwhelming her, and more often than not, she found herself giving in to them. Today was one of those times.

After several fruitless efforts, she finally put aside the landscapes and spent the morning on the brightly colored expressionistic painting that Peter had admired. Stepping back from the canvas, she smiled in satisfaction. There did seem to be something special about the painting. Maybe allowing her imagination to rule her intellect wasn't so bad after all.

She cleaned her brushes, and removed her painter's smock. Feeling unexplainably restless, she began to tidy up the drawers of her dressing table. Anything, she thought, to keep her mind off Peter. In one drawer she discovered a jeweled comb and a pair of matching earrings that had been her mother's. She'd never even considered wearing them before, considering them too ostentatious, but when she dramatically swept one side of her hair back with the comb, the earrings seemed entirely appropriate. Maybe if she unbuttoned the first three buttons of her white blouse and looped a jade silk scarf around her waist to complement her neat black slacks . . . There!

She kicked off her black flats and slipped into a pair of high-heeled jade sandals she found in the back of her closet. She applied a more vivid color of lipstick than she usually wore and, throwing caution to the wind, used a liberal amount of blusher as well. She was reaching for a palette of green eyeshadow when she heard loud voices coming from downstairs.

Hurrying cautiously out the door, Melanie peered over the third-floor balcony. Below, Worth Carroway, Aunt Maddie, and Brown were gathered in the hall, each holding a sheaf of pages, reading aloud in turn. Melanie suppressed a chuckle and stepped out of sight. Her father was working on his historical novel again, demanding that his captive audience act out some of the scenes. She wondered idly what battle he was concentrating on now. The sporadic pace at which her father worked made it a safe guess he wasn't much past the Wars of the Roses, although he'd been writing *The Definitive Chronicle of Wars—Big and Small* off and on ever since she could remember.

Working on the book frequently kept Worth Carroway fully occupied for days, even weeks, at a time. As a child she'd often become so frustrated by his neglect of her in favor of "the book" that more than once she'd planned elaborate ways of destroying his project. Although she'd never had the temerity to actually follow through on her plans, she occasionally still wondered if her father would have been better off if she'd long ago burned the huge pile of manuscript pages.

Melanie was startled out of her reverie by Peter's voice coming from behind her. "Your father asked my opinion of that scene earlier today."

"Peter, must you constantly sneak up on me?"

He shrugged. Then, as his eyes traveled over her, he smiled appreciatively. "You look absolutely marvelous, Mel. Everything in this household seems to be agreeing with you lately." He stepped closer, skimming a thumb along her cheekbone. "I love your hair and . . . your whole outfit."

Melanie flushed. "I was just sort of . . . fooling around," she murmured, backing toward her room. "Wh-what are you doing upstairs?"

He took a step forward, forcing her back against the door, and braced a hand on either side of her. Bending very close, he whispered, "You're becoming a more fascinating woman every day, Mel."

"I-I don't know what you're talking about," she whispered, alarmed by the inner thrill of pleasure his words inspired.

His mouth moved within an inch of hers. "Sure you do," he corrected huskily. "You can't help being aware of the changes that are coming over you. I watched your reaction just now as you watched your family acting out your father's novel. There was no sign of your usual frustration with them, just loving acceptance. I like that. I like everything about you more and more." His eyes darkened as he took in the gaping neckline of her unbuttoned blouse.

A shiver ran through Melanie. The man's ability to imbue the simplest occasion with sexual tension, read the most preposterous things into the most ordinary situation, was simply amazing. Why was he making such a big deal out of a slightly different hairdo, a small change in her attitude toward her family's bizarre carryings-on? Most of all, why did she feel happy he'd noticed all these things, yet also embarrassed? But as he caught her chin in his fingers and lowered his lips to hers, she momentarily forgot her concerns, simply giving in to the swimming sensations his kiss created.

As Peter slowly withdrew his mouth, Melanie gazed into his eyes, seeing both confidence and desire reflected there. Her confusion increased. What in the world was she doing kissing a man who drove her stark raving mad?

Angrily, she pushed him away and turned toward her room. "I've got work to do on my landscapes," she muttered, slipping quickly away.

At two in the afternoon, Melanie realized she had yet to make her first brush stroke on the canvas in front of her. Thinking a change of environment might help, she decided to go downstairs for a quick sandwich. She was halfway to the refrigerator when she wondered if Peter might like something to eat. Good manners, she reasoned, dictated that she ask. After all, no one in the household made much fuss over the noon meal. The family usually just drifted in and out of the kitchen, helping themselves to whatever they wanted. Peter might have been too busy working on Jennifer to remember to eat.

Humming to herself, Melanie quickly assembled two huge sandwiches, poured a couple of tall glasses of iced tea, and carried them on a tray toward the basement stairs. Just as her feet hit the first step, she bounced off an immovable object. As the tray wobbled precariously in her outstretched hand, she knew with unwavering certainty that she was going to fall down the stairs and land in a broken heap at the bottom with mayonnaise dripping from her hair.

But she didn't. Instead, one strong arm encircled her waist while another deftly caught the tray. Her nose was crushed against something fuzzy and blue, her legs pressed against something hard, and her senses inhaled a familiar, distinctly male scent. She was perfectly safe. Also embarrassed. By Peter Valentine. Again. She tilted her head back to look into dark-centered pupils that were still adjusting to the sunlight streaming in the kitchen windows, and sighed.

"You have lint on your nose. From my sweater," he said softly, removing his hand from her waist to flick it off.

Melanie swayed against the doorjamb, disturbingly aware that its hundred-year-old supports didn't feel nearly as secure as Peter's arms. "I—I was just going to have lunch," she muttered, suddenly too shaken to admit she'd been about to ask him to join her.

"In the basement?" His tone was light and teasing.

"Uh—sort of..." Her heart was doing its trip-hammer routine again, even as she silently berated herself for not being in better control of her emotions.

"Ah, I see. Well, I suppose basements have their own peculiar charm." His eyes shifted to the two large sandwiches on the tray he was still holding. "Do you always eat this much for lunch?"

"N-not generally."

"Hmmm... What all's in the sandwiches?"

"Oh, bologna, mayonnaise, lettuce, mustard, tomato slices, breast of turkey—"

"I love breasts," he pronounced, his eyes moving appreciatively to hers.

She looked away. He was impossible! Like the child in the old nursery rhyme, when he was good, he was very, very good, but when he was bad, he was horrid. And terribly appealing...

He continued lazily, "Breasts are the best part, in fact. They're so delicate, delectable..." His voice trailed off meaningfully.

Melanie's breath caught in her throat, and her knees wobbled slightly as she turned back into the kitchen. "Do you want to share lunch or not?" she asked unsteadily, her back to him.

"I thought you'd never ask."

Two days later, Melanie's restlessness got the best of her. She hadn't worked on her landscapes at all. They seemed too much the same old thing. The pleasure she'd always taken in realistically depicting nature had disappeared. To make matters worse, her experiments with abstract forms were now looking very promising, even to her critical eye. A dangerous sign. She must be losing control of her artistic vision. Which was pretty much true of every aspect of her life these days. It was falling apart! She had to put an end to this foolishness, jump off this emotional seesaw.

What she needed was to get away from the mansion—and from Peter. Especially Peter. The ubiquitous Mr. Valentine was driving her crazy with his perceptive observations. It didn't matter where she was or what she was doing, he would suddenly appear, a maddening, all-knowing smile curving his lips.

He didn't even bother to pretend their meetings were coincidental—which, of course, they weren't. He was trailing her. Well, she could be as cagey as he was!

Quickly shedding her painter's smock and slacks, Melanie put on a slim beige skirt, a matching blazer, a cream blouse, and low-heeled pumps. Her reflection told her she looked like her old conservative self again.

She'd go shopping or take in a matinee, she decided, pinning her hair up in a tight bun the way Harris preferred it. And she wouldn't call for the limo. She'd drive herself, roll down the car windows, breathe in the fresh autumn air, and have an uninterrupted day in which to get her thoughts in order. But she'd have to be very careful or Peter would be right behind her.

She descended the stairs cautiously, pausing to listen for Peter, who could be lurking anywhere. No sign of him yet. So far, so good. She tiptoed down the hall, checked over her shoulder one last time to see if the coast was still clear, and reached into the center drawer of the hall table for a set of car keys. She pulled open the front door and—

"Going somewhere?" asked a casual voice behind her.

The keys fell to the floor with a loud clatter. Melanie's shoulders sagged. Damn!

"Where did you come from?" she demanded crossly, turning to fix him with a menacing glare.

Lounging beside a priceless Greek statue, his hands thrust into the pockets of hunter-green cords, he seemed unperturbed by her reaction. Melanie couldn't help comparing Peter's physique with that of the marble god beside him. No doubt about it. Though the statue was a magnificent example of male symmetry, Peter had the more beautiful body. And his was warm with life and vitality. She sighed.

He lifted a knowing brow. "What did you have in mind to do today, Mel?"

His easygoing manner didn't fool her one bit. "I'm just going out," she said firmly. "Maybe shopping, maybe to a movie. Just out."

"Ah, I see. In that case, give me a minute to get one of my people over here to keep an eye on things while I'm gone, and then we can leave."

"We?"

"Certainly. You don't think I would allow you to go off on your own, do you?"

Melanie's lips compressed tightly. "I don't need your permission to leave this house. And I don't want your company. Why don't you just concentrate on doing your job?"

He moved slowly toward her, his eyes traveling from her severely coiffed hair down her neatly dressed body. "Mel, you know part of my job is to keep an eye on you. You also know you can't leave this house without me. It's much too dangerous. Anyway, you can't go out looking like that."

"I beg your pardon?"

"I said—"

"What's wrong with the way I'm dressed?" She was so upset that her words tumbled over one another.

Peter shrugged, his eyes continuing to appraise her. "Nothing, if you prefer the corporate-executive style to the feminine and sexy look. Lord, Mel, that outfit is so bland it could put a board of directors to sleep. And your hair is much too severe, all pulled up in that tight little bun. You're too beautiful a woman to go around dressed like somebody's grandmother."

Melanie flushed crimson, and her lips quivered in indignation. Peter's eyes danced with merry deviltry as she strode toward him and thrust out her chin. "And what would you have me wear, Peter? A low-cut, clinging dress and stiletto heels? Do you want me to let my hair tumble over my shoulders like a . . . a cavewoman? Maybe I could even dispense with underwear!"

Before the last comment was completely out of her mouth, she saw Peter's eyes darken and his lips part slightly as he pulled her into his embrace. She had only a second to register the look of intense desire in his face before he covered her lips with his own. *I don't like him,* Melanie thought, even as she savored the taste and scent of him. *He fascinates me, but he's too bossy, too opinionated, too rude . . .*

The kiss deepened, and her criticisms vaporized into a steamy mist. She found herself surrendering, kissing him back with fervor, making no protest as he loosened her hair and let it fall in a fiery cascade around her shoulders. One hand stole up to untie the bow at her throat, then undo the top two buttons of her blouse. She was aware that tiny bubbles of joy were dancing inside her . . .

The kiss ended finally, but the feeling didn't. Peter flashed a charmingly sensual smile. "Lady, you're dynamite," he said huskily. "If only you'd let go more often. Have the courage to follow your heart." His fingers played with the third button for a moment, then slipped inside her blouse to stroke the bare flesh just above her breast. Her skin felt as if it were on fire.

He was breathing hard. So was she. There was no denying the chemical reaction they sparked in each other. But that could never be enough, could it? It hadn't been with Rip. A few nights of heavy breathing were not a substitute for stability. Even her discovery of Peter's sensitive, caring side was not enough to change her mind about him. After all, Rip had feigned consideration at first, too.

"I know what you're thinking, Mel," Peter said softly. "But believe me, we've got all the ingredients we need to be happy together. Give me a chance to prove to you that—"

She stepped backwards, cutting off his words with an outstretched palm. His hands fell to his side. "You're making me crazy, Peter! First you encourage me to open up, feel less inhibited. Then you become a—a jailer!"

"I'm sorry you feel that way, Mel," he returned calmly, "but I believe that protecting you is crucial—from both a professional and a personal standpoint. I also think we should get to know each other better."

Melanie forced herself to concentrate on his words, not on her weak limbs and reeling senses. "Peter," she began coldly, "what makes you think I'd *want* to have a relationship with a man who thinks I look like a grandmother and who regards my taste in art as worthless? A man who practically makes love to a computer?" Her voice grew louder. "A man who isn't sensible enough to ignore the strange antics of this household, who actually encourages them, even acts as if they're normal?"

She stomped past him on her way back upstairs, her hair flying around her face, one hand holding the neck of her blouse closed, maddeningly aware that her keeper had gotten exactly what he'd wanted: She was in no mood to press the issue of leaving the house now—with or without him.

She was on the second step when Peter answered her in a confident, clear voice. "Because, Mel, I'm the only man who's ever had the guts to tell you the truth and to make you admit it to yourself as well. And you're as crazy about me as I am about you."

Two days later, Melanie completed her abstract painting and spent most of the morning trying in vain to persuade herself to finish her landscapes. And then an irrepressible urge seized her: Today she would take both the abstract painting and her self-portrait to the little gallery in downtown Fort Worth.

For the first time in a long while she didn't stop to question her motives or examine her reasoning; she just followed her instinct. Today was the day to act.

As she wrapped both paintings carefully in brown paper and secured them with twine, she planned her strategy for getting out of the house without Peter's knowing. It would be difficult, but as she pulled on a pair of designer jeans and then wavered momentarily between choosing a cardigan and a cashmere pullover, an idea struck her. A diversionary tactic might solve her problem. If she could divert Peter's attention . . .

Smiling, she tugged the cashmere sweater on over a pink

jersey shirt. Bland, indeed, she thought smugly, tucking the paintings under one arm. Peter Valentine was going to need a new adjective to describe her before the day was over.

Melanie walked casually downstairs and pretended to head to the kitchen, then after looking hastily around, made a last-minute detour to the hall table. Fishing blindly inside the drawer, she retrieved a set of car keys, shoved them into her pocket, retraced her steps toward the kitchen, and strolled casually into the pantry.

She could hear Cook snoring in her quarters on the other side of the door and the sound of Cora twittering into the telephone in the room next to Cook's. Brown was probably camped out by one of the liquor cabinets in the parlor or library. Aunt Maddie and her father were no doubt napping, as they did every afternoon around this time.

Quietly, Melanie opened the metal door of the circuit-breaker panel, ran a finger along the neatly printed tabs indicating which locations each switch controlled, then, un-hesitantly, tripped the breaker to the basement, which housed Jennifer.

Almost as quickly as she'd annihilated Jennifer, Melanie flew from the pantry into the hall and out the front door.

She was free! The day was splendid, one of those mild autumn afternoons that trick one into thinking winter will never come. Brilliant shafts of sunlight streamed through the trees, and a faint aroma of wood smoke filled the air as she kicked up piles of fallen leaves. The merest wisps of clouds curled on the Wedgwood blue horizon...

Oh, how exhilarating it was to be outside, away from Peter's demanding presence! Free to make her way to the four-car garage at the south side of the estate. Free to jump in a car, open the gate, and speed down the open highway! Free to—

"Ooomph!" she exclaimed as someone grabbed her around the waist from behind and sent her flying into a deep pile of leaves. She and her assailant rolled over several times before she landed on her back and found herself staring up into Peter Valentine's blazing eyes, his knees braced on either side of her, his strong hands pinning her wrists to the ground.

"Damn you!" she sputtered. "Let go of me this instant! How dare you!"

"You look great, Mel," he murmured. "Your hair's spilling every which way—those fiery strands mixed in with all these autumn colors. And I love the way you fill out this sweater. Much more attractive on you than a blazer." Before she could avert her head, he was kissing her, slowly, lingeringly, saturating her senses with the feel of his warm mouth, the teasing rasp of his five-o'clock shadow on her cheek. Her eyes flicked open for a moment, catching a glimpse of his bronzed face, the drifting scraps of cloud overhead, the rolling canopy of gray-blue sky, and the multicolored foliage of the trees in the whispering wind. Then her eyes closed again as his lips continued to work their magic. One of his hands moved from her wrist to trace her cheek in a deliberate circular caress.

A small voice at the back of her mind told her to use her freed hand to sock him a good one, but her pleasure-sated senses ignored the order. She had a wonderfully giddy sensation of floating, as if her mind and her body were no longer connected.

At last Peter withdrew his mouth from hers. "Sorry about the tackle, Mel," he said softly. "I just couldn't resist."

Now, the voice nudged—belt him! Her hand lifted, fluttered weakly, then fell back into the leaves. She'd never hit anyone in her life. Whom did she think she was kidding? Besides, how could she hit a man who'd just kissed her so tenderly? Her lips felt swollen as they finally formed a response. "H-how did you know I'd left the house?" Not exactly a sharp retort, she thought shakily.

"I've hooked up a silent alarm system to Jennifer, which works even when the electricity goes off. If the power source fails when someone trips a breaker, for example—an auxiliary battery pack is automatically activated. It's a standard precautionary measure in the security business."

She should have known. Peter Valentine was always one step ahead of her. If only she'd waited until he was nowhere near the basement command center, then sneaked in and thrown a wrench into Jennifer! Taking risks never paid off—at least not for her.

So what was she doing still lying beneath Peter Valentine in broad daylight? "Please get off," she said flatly.

He complied immediately, springing up agilely and pulling her with him. As the ground and her feet met again, she shook her head in an attempt to clear her spinning senses. Everything around her looked so brilliant. It was as if someone had stripped away a filmy glaze and revealed true reality in breathtaking clarity. The trees looked taller, the sun brighter, and the autumn colors more vibrant than she ever remembered. Peter's arm remained around her waist and she wondered dazedly if the world would look as sharp and beautiful when he removed it. Was he the key to the exciting feelings coursing through her, the magician behind the images dancing before her eyes? Or was she simply experiencing a belated reaction to being outside for the first time in days?

"I'm proud of you, Mel," he murmured.

"Proud?" Her voice sounded unnaturally loud to her newly receptive senses.

"Yeah. I'm delighted to see you show some spunk and independence. Not to mention downright deviousness. *You* tripped that breaker, didn't you?" He chuckled, not waiting for an answer and drew her closer. "Proves I've been right about you all along. Deep down, you're a fighter."

How could she tell Peter she wasn't really anything except desperate to escape from his dubious charms? She hardly deserved the compliments he'd just paid her.

"Gorgeous day, isn't it?" he asked, indicating the world at large with a sweep of his arm.

She nodded, wondering when the earth's axis was going to right itself. She still felt off-center, blinded by the dazzling reality of the last few moments.

Peter bent to retrieve her paintings, which had sailed off in different directions when he tackled her, and handed them to her without comment. He headed toward the garage, his arm wrapped tightly around her waist. Somehow her wooden limbs moved in time with his. He turned his face up to the sun and smiled. "An absolutely gorgeous day. I can understand why you wouldn't want to waste it by staying inside."

She blinked. "Can you?" she asked incredulously.

"Sure."

She decided to test Peter's suspiciously complacent attitude. "I'm taking some paintings to a little gallery downtown—to see if they'd be interested in exhibiting them," she announced firmly.

"Good for you, Mel. I hope this is just your first in a long line of important decisions about your future. Maybe you'll be more willing to take chances from now on." He shot her a meaningful glance.

She dragged her gaze from the sun-and-shadowed planes of his face. She was way out of her league with Peter Valentine. He made her feel things that were too frightening. Just being near him was more of a risk than she cared to take. She had learned her lessons well during her marriage to Rip. Walking this kind of a tightrope was insane; there would be no safety net to catch her when she took the inevitable fall.

She pulled free of Peter and walked briskly ahead of him, retrieving the car keys from her pocket. "I'm taking the car, Peter," she warned, in case he was still thinking of stopping her.

"Perfect day for a drive," he agreed, catching up with her as she entered the garage. "I wouldn't expect you to walk, you know. Much too far."

She gave him a patronizing smile.

"I see you even remembered the keys, Mel. You were well prepared this time."

She still didn't trust his casual attitude. He stood at ease outside the large garage, his arms folded across his chest, grinning. Melanie frowned. Something didn't feel right. Why was he suddenly being so cooperative? Well, there was no sense dwelling on it, she decided. She would simply leave—and quickly—before he changed his mind.

She started toward the Mercedes, then remembered she didn't know which set of keys she'd picked up. They might fit the Cadillac or the Rolls or the BMW. After setting her packages on the hood of the sleek silver Mercedes, she examined the keys in her hand. They didn't look the least bit familiar. And then the devastating realization struck her: All of the keys to the family cars had small identification tags hanging from them. These didn't.

"Something wrong, Mel?" Peter asked.

She whirled around. "These keys don't fit any of our cars!"

"Oh?" he asked innocently. "Let me see."

She kept a tight grip on the key ring as Peter gave it a cursory look. "I'm afraid these are the keys to my car," he said.

"Your car?" Melanie bit her lip in frustration.

"No problem, though. You're welcome to drive Baby. Follow me."

Baby? She hurried after Peter, who headed toward a circular area of asphalt in back of the garage. A sinking feeling began to set in; then her heart plummeted to her toes as she caught her first glimpse of "Baby."

"What do you think?" Peter asked cheerfully, patting the hood of a very old, very decrepit London taxi cab. "Isn't she a beaut?"

Melanie opened her mouth, then shut it again. Peter took her arm. "She *was* running like a top," he remarked proudly, leading her toward his car, "but lately she's had a small problem. Probably just those damned valves acting up. When I get time, I'm going to work on the old gal again. I've fixed most of the basics myself, you know."

"Uh—" Melanie began, but failed to complete her sentence as Peter opened the car door, placed her packages carefully in the back seat, and maneuvered her rigid body behind the steering wheel.

He gestured for her to insert the keys in the ignition. "You're all set, Mel."

She looked dazedly at the old-fashioned dashboard. Her gaze wandered to the gearshift, then down to the pedals on the floor. There were three instead of two! "I can't drive this car!" she cried indignantly.

He lifted a brow. "Well, I realize it's not of the caliber you're accustomed to driving, but I assure you that—"

"No," she exclaimed. "It's not that. I can't drive a standard shift! I don't know low from high."

"Hmmm... That *is* a problem."

"You're darned right it is!" she snapped. "I'm going back to the house and get the keys to the Mercedes." She had one foot out the door when Peter thrust an arm in front of her.

"They're not in the hall table drawer, Mel. I decided that was too dangerous a place to leave keys to expensive vehicles. So I've put them... elsewhere."

Melanie gasped. "When did you do that?"

"Right after I realized how accessible they were to just about anybody," Peter answered calmly. "I guess it must have been the day you considered going shopping or to a matinee..."

Melanie bit her lip to keep from screaming. "Then you just go back to the house and get me a set of keys to one of the family cars, Peter," she said between clenched teeth.

He moved in closer to her and bent to get into the driver's seat. "Scoot over, will you, Mel?" She obliged with a scowl, deciding it would be quicker if he drove them back to the house. "Thanks. Now we're all set." He closed the door and pushed a funny-looking button that made all the locks click down. "Central lock control. "I added it myself," he said proudly, turning the key in the ignition. The engine came haltingly to life, and the car jerked forward. Melanie was surprised at how fast it picked up speed. Peter drove past the garage, turned onto the drive that led to the mansion, then, at the last minute, turned off onto the main stretch leading to the gates!

"W-what are you doing?" Melanie sputtered, even as her brain began to register how cleverly he had manipulated her.

"I'm kidnapping you, Mel."

"You're *what!* Let me out of your car this instant, Peter! If this is your idea of a joke, I don't find it very funny!"

He flashed a smile, opened the gates by pushing a button on a remote control, and shot onto the main road.

"Better give me the address of that art gallery," he said pleasantly, roaring past a car that was just turning into the mansion's drive.

Melanie slumped back against the seat in angry defeat.

* * *

The VanZandt Gallery was located on a chic side street in Fort Worth, nestled among several other specialized, exclusive businesses. Peter found the gallery and easily maneuvered the bulky taxi into a parking space near the entrance. He switched off the ignition, pocketed the keys, and turned to face a silently seething Melanie. "You haven't lost your nerve, have you, Mel?" he asked gently, indicating the door to the gallery with a flicker of an eye.

"I didn't have as much as you to start with," she shot back. "You never intended to let me leave on my own, did you, Peter? You just made me *think* you did, which is the most devious, underhanded—"

"Almost as ingenious as your plan to put Jennifer out of commission long enough to escape me," he interrupted smoothly.

"Obviously, yours was the more ingenious of the two plans, since yours succeeded and mine didn't."

He attempted to look modest, but failed. "I just happen to know a little more about security systems than you do, that's all. Anyway, it's too beautiful a day to waste arguing. Let's go inside and find out how good an art critic I am." He hesitated. "Mel, which paintings did you bring?"

She glared at him. How she hated to admit she'd brought the ones he'd most admired. "My self-portrait and the abstract work," she replied grudgingly.

"No unimaginative landscapes?" he teased softly.

"No landscapes," she confirmed.

He grinned with delight, then brushed a kiss across her cheek. "Let's go inside.

As they approached the door to the gallery, a sudden wave of trepidation gripped Melanie. She put a hand on Peter's arm. "I don't plan to use my real name here. Not at first, anyway. If I manage to interest the owner in my work, I want it to be because he admires my talent, not because he wants my family's financial backing for his gallery."

Peter took her hand. "I'm with you all the way," he

assured her. Somehow his support melted away a large share
of the anger she'd felt toward him. Instinctively she en-
twined her fingers with his. As their eyes met, they shared
a moment of understanding.

They entered the gallery, and Melanie's gaze traveled
with interest to the paintings on the off-white walls. The
few pieces of furniture in the room were of excellent quality.
A man who looked to be in his fifties approached them,
wearing an impeccably tailored navy blazer, cream-colored
slacks, and a maroon ascot arranged precisely in the open
neck of a silk shirt.

"Hello," he greeted them pleasantly. "May I help you?"

With Peter at her side and the comforting atmosphere of
the little gallery surrounding her, Melanie felt less nervous.
"I hope so," she said. "I'm an artist, and I'd like to show
the owner some of my work, to see if he'd be interested in
exhibiting it."

"I see," the man answered, tenting his fingers and
peering over them. "Well, I'm always looking for new
talent, Miss—?"

For one desperate moment Melanie couldn't think how
to respond. How foolish not to have made up a name before
now. But Peter came to her rescue in the space of two
heartbeats. "Jones," he supplied.

"Ah . . . Well, won't you have a seat in my office? I'm
Alfred VanZandt, the owner."

Peter shook the owner's hand, introducing himself merely
as Peter, then he and Melanie followed Mr. VanZandt into
an attractively furnished office at the back of the gallery.
They sat down across from him as he settled into a chair
behind a massive desk. Melanie's heart began to pound
frantically in her chest while the man continued to scrutinize
her. Had he recognized her? Or was he wondering why she
was wearing such an obviously expensive cashmere sweater?
Did he think all young artists wore threadbare hand-me-
downs or that all creative people lived in abject poverty?

Surely he wasn't that naive, she told herself. She felt
reassured when he smiled and said, "Well, Ms. Jones, shall
we take a look at what you brought?"

Melanie nodded stiffly and slid the packages onto the polished surface of the desk. It seemed to take her an eternity to unwrap the canvases, but finally she pulled the paintings free of their wrappings and placed them on a table where they caught the light. Peter took her hand as the gallery owner's eyes swept impassively over the self-portrait. He examined it closely, then turned his attention to the abstract painting, repeating the same unemotional scrutiny.

Melanie's grip on Peter's hand tightened, and she concentrated on a spot on the wall above Mr. VanZandt's head. He stood very erect, tapping his fingers on the table where her canvases stood. When he finally spoke, she jumped slightly. "I would be happy to hang both of these in our current exhibition of works by local artists," he said smoothly. Then his mouth broke into a smile. "You're very talented. These paintings demonstrate a finely honed skill as well as a fresh, original spirit. The emotional intensity is . . . quite marvelous. Now, shall we shake hands on our agreement? We can discuss the details later."

Melanie felt slightly dizzy as she stood up. "You have excellent taste, Mr. VanZandt," Peter congratulated him, grinning broadly at Melanie.

He nodded, taking Melanie's outstretched hand. "Yes, I do," he replied matter-of-factly. "But I have to confess that anyone with a minimal knowledge of art would recognize these paintings as the work of an extraordinary talent."

Melanie was beginning to recover as Peter slipped an arm around her waist. "I—I can't thank you enough, Mr. VanZandt," she said with as much dignity as she could muster. "You don't know what this means to me."

"It's a privilege to be able to exhibit such—" Mr. VanZandt paused in midsentence, lifting a hand to his brow. "Wait a minute! I know you! I've been trying to think . . . I've got it!" He snapped his fingers. "You're Melanie Carroway, aren't you? I saw the photographs of your wedding in the society column of the newspaper last year." He began to chuckle, shaking his head. "I knew you looked vaguely familiar when you walked in a few minutes ago, but I simply couldn't recall where I'd seen you until now."

Melanie shot Peter a frantic glance. "But you didn't know who I was when you agreed to take my paintings? I mean, you didn't realize it until after you'd made your decision?" she asked breathlessly.

Mr. VanZandt looked slightly ashamed. "I'm afraid not. Silly of me, I must admit, but I have a poor memory, except when it comes to works of art."

Melanie leaned across the desk to shake the owner's hand. "Thank God for poor memories, Mr. VanZandt! I'll be in touch in the next couple of weeks or so." She seized Peter's arm, urging him through the office door.

Behind them, the confused gallery owner called, "But do you trust me with these paintings? We haven't discussed prices or commission yet."

Over her shoulder, Melanie called gaily, "I trust you, Mr. VanZandt. And that's trust with a capital *T.*"

Chapter

6

"Peter," Melanie began thoughtfully, as they wove their way in and out of Fort Worth traffic, "what would you have done if I could drive a standard shift car?"

He glanced quickly at her, but long enough for Melanie to see that his gaze was clear, sparkling, and determined. "Oh, fiddled with the spark plugs on some pretense or another, maybe pocketed the distributor cap, something that would convince you I needed to be along to keep the car running."

"You're unbelievable," Melanie retorted. "I never had a chance, did I?"

"Nope. On the other hand, Mel, you're about to have some fun."

Her mood had grown mellower since her success at the art gallery, and she admitted that being with Peter today was turning out to be . . . well, not unpleasant, really. In fact, she wondered if she would have had the courage to go inside the VanZandt Gallery without him. Still, she couldn't help being somewhat suspicious. "Uh, what do you have in mind?" she asked carefully.

"You'll see."

He downshifted, swung the car around a sharp curve, and turned into a section of Fort Worth where Melanie had never been. Fifteen minutes later, they lurched into a graveled lot next to a park. "Here we are," he announced brightly. "Ready?" He climbed out of the driver's side, walked around the hood, and opened her door for her.

She allowed herself to be led toward the park, recognizing immediately that this was a neighborhood recreation center. It was Saturday afternoon, and the park was crowded with children of all ages, shapes, and colors.

Peter pulled her by the hand toward a large brick building that had obviously seen better days. A few of the windows had unsightly cracks, the wood trim was in desperate need of painting, and the roof looked as if it could use reshingling. "Ever been to a park, Mel?" he asked.

"When I was a child—with my nanny," she said hesitantly.

"Ah, of course. A manicured park in a more affluent section of town, I'll bet."

"Yes," she admitted, remembering how organized the play there had been compared to the helter-skelter activities taking place around her. Kids were flying kites, bouncing balls, pushing, shoving, shouting, laughing, even wading in a crumbling stone fountain. But they all appeared to be having loads of fun.

They went inside the building, where Peter led her to a long wooden counter cluttered with pamphlets, lost-and-found baskets, stacks of papers, and wire bins full of play equipment. Three walls were a bright magenta; the fourth sported a mural of kids at play. Melanie studied it curiously. It wasn't skillfully painted, but it was warm, sunny, and appealing, perfect for the atmosphere, and it depicted an unsupervised, joyful scene that stood in startling contrast to her memories of stiffly starched gray-haired nannies herding their charges about.

"Hulk!" Peter shouted.

Melanie turned from the mural to see a young man enter the office from a door in back. He wore an army-green T-shirt and was built like a wrestler. "Hey, Peter!" he cried in a deep baritone. "Long time, no see, man!" He leaned across the counter, seizing Peter's outstretched hand in his enormous palm.

"I've been busy," Peter explained. "Working a job."

"Some job," Hulk returned, his eyes sliding appreciatively over Melanie's provocative figure in her tight jeans and cashmere sweater.

Peter grinned. "Yeah. Well, what can I say? Some fringe benefits are better than others. By the way, meet Melanie Carroway."

Melanie was about to explain that she wasn't anyone's "fringe benefit" when Hulk's huge hand engulfed hers in a surprisingly gentle grip. "Hi, gorgeous! I'm George Adams, but everyone calls me Hulk, for obvious reasons." Melanie cast a furtive glance at his powerful biceps. "Nice to meet you, Melanie. From what Peter's been telling me on the phone, I've gotten the impression that you're a very special lady."

"Be quiet, Hulk, before you destroy the reputation for being carefree that I've so carefully built," Peter teasingly chastised.

Melanie was busy pondering Hulk's comments. Peter had discussed her with a close friend? But she didn't have much time to contemplate why before Peter thrust a bright red and green kite into her hand, passed a stack of bills to Hulk, and steered her out the door.

"Thanks, Peter," Hulk called. "Don't be a stranger."

Peter gave a wave over his shoulder as they walked toward a far corner of the park. "Ever flown a kite before?" he asked.

"I'm afraid not," Melanie admitted. "Listen, Peter, why did you have to pay so much for this kite? I saw a sign that said the play equipment was free."

He shrugged. "Let's call it a donation, Mel."

Melanie looked around her and realized this park was undoubtedly run almost solely on contributions, and with the help of volunteer workers. It was situated in an impoverished area, and she guessed it was the only place where the kids could hang out besides the streets. Peter, she noticed, had changed the subject, as if to deter further discussion of his generosity.

When they reached a relatively unoccupied area of the

park, he said, "Okay, Mel, flying a kite is really a cinch, but you have to watch me very carefully. The trick lies in letting the string out gradually as the wind catches and lifts the kite. And, of course, you've got to run at the same time, watching out for tree branches and park benches."

"Peter, I really don't think I'm up to this," Melanie began, remembering how impossibly uncoordinated she'd been as a kid.

"Nonsense, Mel," he chastised. "You'll do fine—and have a great time, too. Now watch me."

Effortlessly he held up the kite and sprinted across the grass, letting out the string and allowing the kite to rise gently into the sky. Melanie gazed with rapt attention at the beautiful sight of his finely honed body and the brightly colored kite tugging on the string. As a fresh gust of wind lifted the kite even higher, Peter ran back to her with a triumphant grin. "See? Nothing to it. Now, why don't you try?" he said, reeling in the string.

"Oh, no, Peter. I'm really not ready yet." She held her hands behind her back. "Show me one more time, and I'm sure I'll have it down pat."

As he finished bringing down the kite and took off across the lawn once more, she decided that kite flying might not be so bad, after all, as long as she could watch Peter's athletic body perform. Was it possible to be infatuated with a man merely because of the way his hair grew tousled in the breeze? Because of the way his torso twisted in midair and his legs stretched beneath his form-fitting jeans?

Finally he insisted she take her turn. "Just think about what you're doing and ignore me," he advised, apparently oblivious to her painful self-awareness as her breasts bounced and her feet stumbled. But when she met his encouraging smile, she was able to forget her self-consciousness and concentrate on the task at hand. Soon she gave herself up to the glorious day, to the joy of running pell-mell across the cool grass, her hair blowing around her face, the kite swooping and soaring behind her. With a giggle she skipped around a flower bed and nimbly dodged a park bench. What terrific fun she was having!

Suddenly the string grew so taut in her hand that it threatened to snap. She abruptly halted and turned to stare in dismay. The tail of the kite had gotten caught in a tree branch! Oh, well, no problem, she thought, waving Peter away and calling out, "I can free it."

Holding the string between her teeth, she removed her shoes, and tossed them carelessly to one side. The sunwarmed grass and crisp leaves pleasurably prickled her bare feet as she looked up at the badly tangled tail and the diamond-shaped body dancing in the breeze.

No problem. She'd just climb up there and unsnarl the mess. She paused for only a few seconds, deciding how to begin, then noticed a notch in the bark that looked as if it would make a good foothold. She secured the string in her mouth, struck her right foot in the notch, and began to haul herself up the trunk. Though it wasn't as easy as she'd anticipated, she felt good about her slow, steady progress—until she reached the limb that ensnared the kite's tail, patiently unwound it so that the kite floated free, and turned to climb back down.

My goodness! Had she really climbed this far? Melanie blinked, saw that the ground hadn't gotten any closer, and lowered herself to the fork where the branch met the tree, clinging to the trunk with one hand and the branch with the other. She wasn't frightened, she told herself, just exercising caution. When she was ready, she'd climb back down.

Below her a crowd of children had gathered, including some kids who were rude enough to point at her. I'll just reassure them I'm okay, Melanie thought, then maybe they'll go away. Removing the roll of kite string from her mouth very carefully so as not to disturb her precarious balance, she looped part of it around her waist several times and called down, "Hi! Great view from up here."

"Should we call for help or something, lady?" one grubbyfaced youngster yelled. "I mean, should we call the fire department or police? That's what we did when my cat got stuck in a tree."

"I'm not *stuck*," Melanie assured him. "I'm just resting."

"She's stuck, all right," another kid said, rolling his eyes.

"She just doesn't want to admit it."

"Yeah, adults are like that," a little girl agreed in a shrill, patronizing voice.

"Mel! Are you going to stop clowning around and come down here or not?" a much deeper voice shouted.

Melanie peered cautiously down. Peter was smiling confidently up at her. "I'm getting hungry," he said, flashing her a broad wink. "And besides, I can't stand here all day with my neck craned in this position, watching you have fun. Just reverse the steps you used to get up in the tree, Mel, and stop scaring all these kids."

She started to hurl an insult at him, then realized he was trying to help her save face. Reverse the steps, he'd said. That seemed elementary. The trick was in getting her rigid body to cooperate. "I like it up here," she yelled. "Really."

"I know you do," Peter agreed. "But I'm ready for a hot dog and a cool drink. Aren't you?"

Actually, she was ready for a safety net, but she didn't want to prove that Peter's faith in her was misplaced. Very slowly she wriggled around until she could dangle a foot, searching for a place to put it. Her bare toes found a foothold on the gnarled trunk. She let her other foot down experimentally. Then she began to inch her way down—literally. Below, she could hear Peter chatting with the kids, saying, "She does this kind of thing all the time. Loves heights. She's got a real sense of adventure. This was the only tree in the park she hadn't climbed. Made up her mind today was the day."

Buoyed by his encouragement, Melanie kept at her task, concentrating on Peter's outrageous lies instead of her incipient attack of vertigo. Finally she let her feet touch the ground. She turned around, one hand still braced against the tree, her legs trembling, and smiled crookedly. "My, that was fun," she exclaimed weakly.

"That's my girl." Peter smiled proudly at her. "Best little tree-climber in Forth Worth!" He slung an arm around her shoulders, helping to steady her disoriented body. "Anytime you kids want tips about scaling trees, just ask the expert here."

The gang of children stared at her with curiosity until the tallest stepped forward. "My mom doesn't know how to climb trees," he announced flatly. "And she must be at least as old as you are."

Peter barely managed to stifle a chuckle. "Really?" Melanie asked sweetly. "Heavens, she doesn't have much time left to learn, does she?"

The boy shook his head gravely before giving her a wide smile, exposing two missing teeth. "Nope. She's even got a couple of gray hairs. But maybe you could teach her how to climb a tree sometime."

The rest of the children nodded enthusiastically, several echoing the boy's sentiments. Then they wandered away, resuming their play.

"Mel, you've just earned yourself a place in this park's folklore," Peter said wryly. "You're on your way to becoming a neighborhood heroine." He turned her to him, cupping her face in his hands. Huskily, he added, "You were so uninhibited, so spontaneous when you were running with the kite. You're beautiful, and if we weren't in the middle of this crowded place, I'd *show* you exactly how I feel."

Melanie's head was starting to clear now that she was safely on the ground, and her fear was once again giving way to joy. With a start, she realized she hadn't felt this carefree since she was a child—and then, only on rare occasions. And as she gazed into Peter's admiring eyes, she suddenly knew everything she was experiencing was somehow connected to his magic influence.

Peter insisted they celebrate Melanie's kite-flying adventure at a refreshment stand. Three hot dogs, a box of popcorn, and two colas later, Melanie was glad she hadn't consumed all of that food *before* she'd climbed the tree. Sighing, she leaned against the park bench, crossing her hands over her full stomach. "Is it nap time yet?" she asked half-seriously.

Peter fixed her with a look of mock horror. "Certainly not. We need to exercise to get our blood flowing again, put color in our cheeks, start our hearts pumping—"

"Vigorous activity is greatly overrated." Melanie yawned. "Sleeping, on the other hand, is supposed to be great for revitalizing . . ."

Peter cocked his head, looking off into the distance. Then he stood abruptly, pulling her up with him.

"What do you have in mind, Peter?" she asked suspiciously, wary of the gleefully mischievous expression on his face.

"Baseball," he announced.

"Baseball!" She moaned. "Oh, no, Peter, I don't know the first thing about—"

He pretended not to hear her protestations as he dragged her toward a baseball diamond on the west side of the park. A couple of kids were just walking off the field, and the other players were glaring after them.

"Hey, this is the ninth inning! Come on, Johnny! Freddie!" the red-haired pitcher wailed. "You can be a little late just this once."

The two boys shook their heads in unison. "Nope," one of them called over his shoulder. "Our mom will ground us if we're late again."

The pitcher threw his cap on the ground in disgust. "Great. Bottom of the ninth, we're only one run up on the other team, and you two are goin' home!" he shouted angrily.

Peter pulled Melanie along as he strode toward the disgruntled redhead. "Need a couple of players?" he asked cheerfully.

"You got two kids that could play on our team?"

"I'm afraid not," Melanie said, relieved.

"What about us?" Peter replied.

"Aw . . . You're just adults!"

"Sorry about that," Peter apologized, chuckling. "But we appear to be your only volunteers at the moment."

The boy retrieved his cap, shoved it onto his head, and appraised Melanie skeptically. "She any good?" he asked, hooking a thumb in her direction.

"No," Melanie answered quickly.

"Yes," Peter corrected. "Or she will be after I explain the game to her. She's an artist, has great hand-eye coordination."

"Put her in the outfield, then," the pitcher said, resigned. "You take third base."

A few minutes later, Melanie found herself in center field, glove in hand, peaked cap on her head. Peter had just finished explaining the rules of the game to her. It seemed relatively simple, actually, except for the part about where to throw the ball in case one came her way. Of course, there was the added difficulty of catching it first. But Peter had said that was elementary. She should just keep her eye on the ball and use two hands.

Two pop flies later, one caught by the shortstop and the other by the second baseman, Melanie decided that playing her position was a breeze. Why in the world did baseball teams even need people in the outfield? Nobody ever hit a ball this far. She started to yawn, sleepy from all of the food she'd eaten when the splintering crack of a bat and the frantic cries of the left fielder brought her back to attention. "Back up! Back up! It's yours!"

Looking upward, she saw with dismay that a high, arcing ball was headed in her direction. Far away, she heard Peter shouting unintelligible encouragement from third base. Keep your eye on it, he'd said earlier. She squinted into the setting sun, moving backwards as it became apparent that the ball was going to be beyond her reach if she didn't. She was dimly aware of a cacophony of excited cries from the opposing team's dugout. "It's going over! A homer for sure! All right!"

Almost to the fence, the ball began a slow descent. Then, inexplicably, it seemed to pick up speed. All of a sudden it was plummeting straight toward her nose. Melanie made a quick decision: Forget Peter's rules for catching a ball. She was going to be killed! She shut her eyes and crossed her wrists with the glove, palm outward, covering her face. Maybe, if she was very lucky, she'd only suffer a mild concussion.

A resounding smack startled her, and she fell onto her bottom as her spinal cord whacked into the fence. Instinctively, she clamped her other hand over whatever had fallen into the glove. She was afraid to move. A wild chorus of cheers went up, and moments later, she felt herself being lifted onto someone's shoulders. She lowered her hands, opened her eyes, looked into her glove, and saw a ball. Good Lord, was that *the ball?*

"You're a hero, Mel!" Peter shouted proudly, tilting his head back to see her face as he carried her among her cheering teammates.

"I—I didn't know where to throw it," she cried over the loud confusion.

"You didn't have to," the pitcher yelled, jumping up and down excitedly. "There were two outs already. You caught what could have been the tying run. Heck, their batter never even made it to second."

"Should I apologize to the other team?" she asked worriedly.

Peter laughed. "Nope. But I tell you what, I'll buy everyone an ice cream cone—losers, too! How's that sound?"

Melanie forgot she had been stuffed to her eyeballs in junk food earlier. She conveniently didn't remember being nearly frightened out of her skull moments ago. She simply relished her success. She'd caught the ball! Helped her team win the game! Oh, what a feeling! "Make mine a double scoop. Chocolate chip!"

Chapter
7

MELANIE SUSPECTED SHE was having too much fun for her own good. When she and Rip first met, she'd experienced this same kind of uninhibited, world-at-my-feet feeling. And look at where that had gotten her. Back to square one. Why in the world had she ever allowed Peter to talk her into climbing back onto the merry-go-round again? The dizzying whirl would inevitably end, and then Peter would either move on to a new challenge or find another woman who didn't need so much persuading.

She glanced at his profile in the dim light of the car's interior. He looked totally relaxed and at peace with himself. Well, why not? He probably didn't give much thought to tomorrow or to the inevitable consequences of this little flirtation. No doubt he never got so seriously involved with a woman that he had to worry about having his heart broken.

"Don't start throwing up imaginary barriers, Mel," Peter warned matter-of-factly, not taking his eyes off the road. "The evening isn't over, and neither are we."

She stared at him in disbelief. The man was uncanny. Nerve-racking. Irresistible. The wind had blown his hair into tumbled waves, while the sun had bronzed his cheeks to an even darker hue. He was so totally alive, so vibrant, so completely in control.

"Here we are," he said, swinging his old car to the curb

in a part of downtown Forth Worth that looked only vaguely familiar to Melanie. "This is one of my favorite haunts, a place where people can feel free to be themselves."

Once again he moved too quickly for her to protest. They were going down the steps to the basement bar before she finally managed to say, "Peter, I can't go inside. I must look awful. My face feels sunburned, my hair is all over the place, and I'm dressed much too casually to—"

"You look terrific, Mel," he assured her. "Your cheeks are glowing, your hair is soft and full . . ." He smiled. "I've never seen you look more beautiful or more relaxed." He captured her mouth in a brief kiss, draped an arm around her shoulders, and thrust open the door to the bar.

The small, crowded space was lit by multicolored globes that hung from the ceiling. Tables and booths full of people surrounded a dance floor in the center of the room. A long bar ran the length of one wall. Behind it, bartenders and waitresses were busy fixing drinks and juggling trays. Peter guided Melanie toward a large table in the back, where several laughing men and women were gathered.

"Peter!" cried a young woman in a snug pink sweater. "Where've you been keeping yourself?" She planted an exuberant kiss on his cheek. Melanie was not prepared for the surge of jealousy she experienced, but she forced herself to smile at the pretty, self-confident brunette, who gave her a friendly, curious glance.

"I've been working," Peter explained good-naturedly. "Minding the store."

A chorus of groans went up from the table; then everyone started talking at once. Melanie couldn't follow much of what they were saying. The ten or so people all seemed to know Peter intimately, and talked so fast that what with the loud music and the other bar patrons' chatter, she could catch only snatches of phrases: "Missed seeing you." "Molly and Gary couldn't make it tonight." "There's a party next weekend at Susan's new condo."

Peter responded amiably, keeping an arm around Melanie's shoulders. Then one of the men dragged two chairs over, and she found herself sitting between Peter and the bouncy brunette. He held up a silencing hand. "Hey! Quiet down for a minute, will you? Everybody, I'd like you to meet Melanie Carroway."

The talking ceased. Heads turned toward her. Melanie froze. She'd endured so many evenings with Rip and his wild crowd that she knew what would inevitably come next: pretended, polite interest and then, as the evening wore on, she would become no more important to these carefree people than the woodwork. But to her astonishment, the group responded enthusiastically to Peter's introduction. Everyone began to speak at once, welcoming her, giving their names, and treating her as if she were one of them, not an outsider. Their warmth made it easy to flash a genuine smile in each person's direction.

Pink Sweater leaned over, put a hand on her arm, and said, "I'm Jody Green. And I'm absolutely delighted Peter's found someone like you."

Blinking, Melanie turned to seek out Peter and realized he was at the bar ordering drinks. She shifted her attention back to Jody, who was regarding her with frank admiration. "I—I'm not exactly Peter's date," Melanie explained haltingly.

Jody laughed. "Honey, whatever you want to call it is fine with me, but I've never seen Peter look at any woman the way he looks at you. He's told us how special you are to him, and we've all been dying to meet the mystery woman in his life."

Melanie cleared her throat. "Well, I haven't known him very long."

Jody took a long swallow of her beer and said, "Those of us who know him well have always figured once he found the right woman, time wouldn't matter. Peter goes after what he wants. Take the community recreation center, for instance, where we all met. The place was almost closed down a year ago. Each of us has been a volunteer in one capacity or another, but we'd run out of funds and hope. Then Peter joined us and turned things around. He spent hours raising funds and doing painting and carpentry. There's still a lot of work to be done, but with his help, we'll finish it all in another few months or so. Peter's incredible!"

"Why do you think he picked that particular project?" Melanie asked.

Jody shrugged. "He loves kids." A frown crossed her face. "It's hard to get him to talk about himself, but from what I've pieced together, I think he had a tough childhood. I suspect that when he was a kid, a neighborhood recreation center like ours helped fill some of the voids in his life."

"How does he find so much time to devote to the rec center? I mean, he has a job and—"

"Boy, you really don't know much about him, do you?" Jody asked, but her tone was kind. "He doesn't just work for that security outfit, Melanie. He's the head Fred, in charge of the whole shooting match. He has several agencies around the country. He started them all, and as soon as one was self-sufficient, he'd move on to launch another. He's a very highly respected security consultant, one of the best, I understand. But he has a full-time staff, so he rarely has to go out into the field himself. That gives him the freedom to arrange his own schedule."

Melanie pondered this information silently. If Peter didn't usually go out and work in the field, then why had he chosen to do so for her family? And if he was doing so well financially, why did he drive such an old car? Under normal circumstances, she would never have had the nerve to press Jody for more facts, but she was suddenly consumed by a burning desire to find out as much as she could. "Jody," she continued, "somehow I got the impression Peter occasionally handles clients himself."

Jody chuckled. "Oh, yeah, I guess so. He jokes that every once in a while he likes to make sure he hasn't lost his touch. But after he proves that he can penetrate a client's security system, he usually turns the case over to one of his employees." She took another sip of beer, then broke into a smile. "I'm sure you've seen that awful old car he's always working on. Calls it his undercover cruiser. What a monstrosity! But Peter says it has sentimental value because it was the first car he ever owned."

So Peter had a sense of loyalty . . . at least to things.

Melanie started to ask Jody what else she knew about him, but just then he returned, handing her a tall glass of foamy beer and sitting down beside her. "Since we're going to be here for a while, I thought you might prefer this to the hard stuff," he said.

Melanie had tasted beer only a few times in her life and hadn't particularly cared for it, but she thanked him and tilted the glass to her lips with what she hoped appeared to be practiced ease. The beer tasted as she remembered— like soapy dishwater. With effort, she managed to keep from choking.

The free-flowing conversation began again among Peter's friends, but Melanie felt comfortable, even included. She was particularly grateful that Peter didn't refer to her as the Carroway heiress. When someone asked her what she did, she simply said she was an artist. She was delighted when Peter added that she was a damned good one, stressing that she'd just had two paintings accepted by the VanZandt Gallery. Everyone at the table congratulated her, raising their glasses in a toast.

One of the men at the table said he liked to dabble in art in his spare time, but that his everyday job was in insurance. Jody, she discovered, was a legal secretary for a well-known firm in Fort Worth. The others included a teacher and an assistant vice-president of a bank.

When a haunting melody came over the speaker system, which Melanie recognized as the latest release of a young male singer who specialized in love songs, Peter seized her hand and led her onto the dance floor. She started to assume the traditional position for ballroom dancing, but he gently guided her hands to his shoulders.

"I like slow dancing better this way," he murmured into her ear, drawing her closer. "Don't you?" His voice was low and throbbing, like the music.

"Mmmm . . ." was all Melanie could utter. Peter had tilted his head so that his lips were buried against her neck. Her breasts were crushed into his hard chest, and her thighs pressed against his as they swayed back and forth. They weren't so much dancing as embracing each other, she realized. She felt as if she and Peter were the only two people on the floor, the only ones aware of the song's true rhythm and meaning. A hot flush tingled through her and she surrendered herself to the song and the moment.

The music ended and they returned to the table, their arms still around each other. When they sat down, Peter's hand drifted to her knee. All of a sudden she was terribly thirsty. She drank the rest of her beer in hasty swallows, surprised to discover how much better it tasted than it had earlier. Someone ordered a pitcher and refilled her glass. Beneath the table, Peter's hand was moving slowly up her thigh, though he was apparently immersed in conversation. Melanie took another long sip of beer. My, it had grown hot inside the bar. Or was she simply experiencing what Peter had once called "body heat"?

The lusty strains of rock music began, and several people at the table got up to dance. Peter's hand moved to the small of her back as he guided her onto the floor again. "Peter," she said desperately, trying to make herself heard over the noise, "I don't know how to dance this kind of—"

"Just do what I do," he shouted, slipping his hands around her waist and beginning to move to the music. What could she do? she wondered as his fingers worked their way beneath her sweater. She couldn't just stand there like a wooden dummy. Around them, everyone was dancing much like Peter, their hips gyrating in perfect time to the music. Peter danced as he did everything else—with perfect coordination and seemingly effortless grace. Yet there was a sexy, restless energy in his movements . . .

Making an effort, Melanie began to shift her feet in time to the music. Peter smiled encouragement and spun around in a complicated series of steps that left her dizzy and bewildered. Again she tried to do what he did. She executed an experimental turn, swinging her hips cautiously. It felt good. She became a little bolder in her movements, feeling freer, less inhibited. A passing waitress offered her a beer from a tray, which she declined, deciding she'd already had enough. But several people around her accepted glasses, sloshing beer over the rims.

Peter began a sideways motion, bumping her hip slightly. Laughing, she bumped him back. This was fun! She felt the hard thrust of his thigh against hers; then he spun away before returning to repeat the action. The next time he swung close, she caught his arm and pressed her lips to his ear, shouting, "This is much better than baseball." He rewarded her with a dazzling smile and a particularly intimate bump.

When the dance ended, Melanie found herself wishing it hadn't as she and Peter sat back down at the table. She loved dancing with him, touching him, being with him . . . He released her fingers for a moment to steady a full pitcher of beer that one of his male friends was awkwardly attempting to pour from. Without thinking, Melanie allowed her hand to drop to his thigh. His head jerked around, and he regarded her in delighted surprise. She smiled warmly, sending him an implicit message with her eyes: *This feels so right*. He nodded almost imperceptibly, then quickly covered her hand with his own as if he were afraid she'd change her mind and withdraw her intimate touch.

"Anyway, Carl was baby-sitting a friend's dog, a Doberman, and Carl, as you all know is *terrified* of large dogs. But he owed this guy, see . . ." Realizing that Jody was in the middle of a story, Melanie forced herself to pay attention, reluctantly shifting her gaze from Peter to the animated young woman.

"Actually, he owed him *money,* not just a favor," Jody continued, "or Carl would never have taken the dog into his apartment." Everyone laughed appreciatively. "So to make a long story short, the Doberman took an instant dislike to Carl—the feeling was mutual, believe me—and held him prisoner in his own bedroom closet for the whole evening! When Carl's friend came to reclaim his dog, the poor man had to get the building super to let him in because Carl couldn't come to the door. All he could do was scream bloody murder from inside his closet!"

Jody collapsed into chuckles, along with the rest of the group. "My brother," she explained to Melanie. "Stuff like that could only happen to Carl."

"Oh, I don't know," Melanie returned impulsively. "My

family has a dog of rather dubious character, and I'm afraid he's allowed to do pretty much as he pleases. Once my aunt fed a meringue-topped pie to McNurty—"

"McNurty!" everyone cried.

"Well," Melanie continued, pleased that the group was already seeing humor in her story, "McNurty devoured the entire pie in record time, then ran off before my aunt could wipe the meringue from his mouth. By the time she caught up to him, he'd cornered the maid, who was standing in the middle of a bed screaming that McNurty had rabies!"

As Peter's friends let out another roar of laughter, Melanie felt flushed with happiness. It was so much fun to be the center of attention and to make everyone laugh. She glanced at Peter, whose eyes reflected both pride and amusement.

Somebody at the opposite end of the table cried, "Come on, folks, time to boogie!" Everyone rose, clapping their hands to the frantic beat of hard rock. As her feet hit the polished dance floor, Melanie could hardly contain her joy and excitement. Was Peter's intense gaze what was causing her to feel as special as Jody and Hulk had hinted she was to him? Or was she happy just because she fitted so easily into the group? Whatever the source of her sudden abandon, she reveled in it, tossing her head and swaying her hips, shimmying daringly among the other dancers.

Before she realized what was happening, Peter's friends and some of the other bar patrons had formed a gyrating circle around her and with shouts of approval were urging her to try even wilder dance steps. The music's tempo increased. The clapping grew more enthusiastic. She executed a whirling spin, enjoying the feel of her hair swinging around her face, captivated by the attention of the swaying crowd. Everyone was watching her. She, Melanie Carroway, who'd never been in the center of anything in her entire life, was the life of the party!

But the best part of the solo performance was Peter's reaction. Although he was clapping along with the rest of the group, his eyes following her every movement, it was his smile that ignited the blazing heat inside her, that made her feel as if she could go on dancing forever...

When the music ended, Melanie threw both arms high into the air in a triumphant salute. Her hair hung around her face in damp tendrils, and her chest was heaving from exertion. She took two tottering steps toward Peter, who pulled her against him, cushioning her head on his shoulder. "You were wonderful, Mel," he whispered, "but I think it's time to go. You've had a very full day."

She turned her flushed face up to him, her bleary vision dimly registering that the colored lights seemed very far away. A wave of sudden and total exhaustion almost overwhelmed her, and she staggered slightly. Peter immediately tightened his hold on her. He was saying something, but she was having difficulty concentrating on his words. Even his smile seemed out of focus. If only she could summon a little energy, she and Peter could dance some more...

He guided her back to the table, where she heard him telling the group good-bye, that they'd see them again soon. Why did the evening have to end? She was having such a wonderful time. A protest formed on her lips, but she couldn't seem to get the words out. Her mouth felt fuzzy, her arms and legs like limp spaghetti.

Several members of the group were telling her how much fun she was and that they'd like to get together again before long. Someone said, "Hey, Peter, give her a little hair of the dog in the morning if she needs it."

What in the world was he talking about? Melanie wondered. Did it have something to do with McNurty? Jody kissed her cheek, mumbled something about seeing her again soon, and then she was being led out the door into the cool night air. She turned around once, gave an exhausted wave to her new friends, and fell heavily against Peter's shoulder.

Somehow she found herself in the car snuggled against him. His elbow kept brushing her breast as he shifted gears. The windows were all down, and a brisk night breeze began to cool her hot face. "Feels good," she murmured.

"My elbow feels good?" Peter asked huskily.

"That, too," she whispered. "Especially that."

"Mel, I'm sorry I didn't realize sooner how exhausted

you were. You're probably not used to beer at all."

She patted his thigh. "I had a perfectly terrific time. Thanks to you." Her eyelids felt so heavy, it was hard to keep them open. "Terrific," she emphasized sleepily.

"Next time, we won't try to cram so much into one day, Mel," Peter assured her.

She yawned. "Mmmm . . . You know, Brown ought to try dancing. It'd limber up his arthritic joints, and he'd be too busy to drink."

"There were some people on the dance floor who proved just the opposite tonight," he reminded her gently.

The point of his comment escaped her. She was so ridiculously tired . . . "Peter, I've had such a good time with you. Tell you what. As repayment for all of the fun you've shown me, I'm going to include you in the portrait of Aunt Maddie and McNurty."

"I'd consider that an honor, Mel. But you don't need to repay me for anything. All I want is a chance to show you how much I—"

"You're the best kite flier I know, Peter," she interrupted groggily. "And the best dancer. And the best third baseman. But most of all, you're the very best kisser . . . in the world . . ." Her voice trailed off. She'd just rest her eyes for a little bit. Later on, maybe she'd be able to tell him he was also the sexiest, most desirable . . . Melanie's head slumped onto Peter's chest, and her eyes flickered momentarily before they closed. Her last conscious thought was that they seemed to be taking the wrong road back to the mansion.

The warmth of the sun on her face, and the realization that her head was resting on something firm but comfortable awakened Melanie. She sat up suddenly, looked around, and saw that she wasn't home in bed. She'd been sleeping against Peter's chest—in his car!

He stirred, stretched, and cradled the nape of her neck in his hand. "Good morning, sunshine," he greeted her huskily.

She caught a glimpse of herself in the rearview mirror and blinked. Her hair was in wild disarray and her face was definitely sunburned. Looking down, she saw that her clothes were hopelessly rumpled. "Good morning," she returned cheerfully, wondering why she felt so much better than she looked.

Peter sat up straighter. "Yesterday was wonderful, wasn't it, Mel?"

"Wonderful," she agreed happily, checking her reflection in the mirror again. Actually, she didn't look so bad, she decided. The color in her cheeks was flattering, and her hair tumbled around her face in a casually tousled style that many women spent a lot of money trying to achieve. And she felt completely rested. Except for a dry mouth, she was fine. No, make that better than fine. She felt marvelous!

Peter encircled her shoulders with an arm. "You know, Mel, I think the kidnapping went off very well, considering the fact that I've never planned one before."

Melanie wrinkled her brow. *"Planned?"* she repeated incredulously, spinning around to face him, her voice rising slightly. "Wait a minute, Peter. Are you saying you deliberately—"

"Deliberately and carefully," he interrupted smugly, tracing the strong lines of her chin, his brow arched in amusement. "I knew it would be just a matter of time before you tried to escape the increasing frustrations of our relationship, Mel. As a matter of fact, the idea first occurred to me the day I stopped you from going shopping. I decided that the next time you attempted to escape I would whisk you off somewhere away from the mansion, where you could relax and come to accept me for the all-around charming guy I am." He smiled winningly. "It worked, too."

Melanie crossed her arms over her chest and fixed him with a meaningful glare. "You must have worked awfully hard at making sure I was *continually* frustrated, Peter— practically up to the panting stage. All of that effort must have been exhausting, as well as time-consuming."

Peter pulled her closer, his smug expression replaced by one of complete sincerity. "Mel, I didn't have to *work* at anything where you're concerned—except figuring out the best way to get you to myself so we could really get to know each other, have some time to explore our mutual attraction. As for the 'panting stage,' honey, if it's any consolation, I've taken more cold showers since meeting you than I ever have in my life!"

Melanie grinned. She couldn't help it. For one thing, she was happier than she'd ever been; for another, after hearing Peter out, she was convinced he was more dedicated than devious. And that thought was irresistibly flattering. Imagine someone like Peter Valentine pursuing her because he found her attractive! Because he wanted to get to know her better! Because she drove him so crazy he had to take cold showers! Her smile deepened. No man had ever told her she played such havoc with his libido.

"Mel?" Peter's voice had lost some of its earlier confidence. "Tell me that silent smile means you're as happy as I am."

Melanie had been considering whether she should deflate Peter's ego just a little. After all, he'd been so sure all along that she'd open up to him if he could just prove they really shared something special. But maybe her silence had been enough. Besides, it would be silly to punish a man for being absolutely right. "I'm very happy, Peter," she confessed. "But I am mildly curious as to why we're in the middle of nowhere," she added, looking out the window.

They were parked on a sandy country road. A cotton field lay to her left, and to her right were bushy clumps of mesquite. There was no traffic, nor any houses in sight.

Peter cupped her face in his hands. "We spent the night in the car, Mel. After we left the bar, I drove sort of aimlessly, not wanting the evening to end." His thumb brushed her cheekbone in a fleeting caress. "Do you feel rested enough to take a walk?"

She was still considering the first part of what he'd said: *Not wanting the evening to end.* The same way she'd felt. "Hmmm?" she asked vaguely.

"We need to find somewhere to eat breakfast and then find a tow service," he said softly.

"Tow service?" she repeated, not concentrating on what he was saying so much as on the tingling pressure of his fingers on her skin.

"Yeah." He looked at his watch. "Let's see. It's six-thirty now. I guess the car stopped running around midnight. Damned valves again. I could fix the problem if I had my tools with me, but they're all back at the mansion."

Melanie was amazed that she was relatively unconcerned by Peter's revelation. In fact, the only cloud hanging on her otherwise sunny horizon was worrying about how her family would react when they discovered she'd been out all night and still hadn't returned home. "Let's just find a phone and call my father so he won't panic," she suggested.

"No problem, Mel. He and your aunt were napping yesterday when I kidnapped you, but I left a message for them with Brown. I explained that we might be gone the entire weekend. Then, I asked one of my men to protect the mansion while I was away. You probably didn't notice, but we passed him driving toward the gate as we were pulling out onto the road."

In the brilliant sunshine streaming through the car window, Peter's eyes reflected a kaleidoscope of colors, as varied as the different aspects of his personality. How fascinating! Everything about Peter Valentine was fascinating. "How in the world could you accomplish all of that in such a short time?" she asked with wonder.

He attempted to look humble, but failed. "Easy. Since Jennifer alerted me the moment you went out the door, I knew I had time to make a quick phone call to my agency, talk to Brown, and still intercept you before you left the grounds. Especially since I knew you didn't have access to any car keys except Baby's. There's a little trick in starting her, you see. You have to jiggle the ignition a certain way."

Melanie punched him lightly in the arm. "So it didn't matter whether I could drive a standard shift or not, did it? And all that talk about fiddling with spark plugs and distributor whatever was just that—talk! I would never have gotten the car started!"

"That pretty well sums it up, Mel," he admitted. "But don't blame me for being good at what I do. After all, your father wanted the best."

"Do you have any other confessions to make before we begin hiking back to civilization?" Melanie asked playfully.

"I'm saving them for later," he promised, opening the car door.

His words sent a small thrill of anticipation through her. "I'll hold you to that," she warned softly, following him out his side of the car. He locked Baby, pocketed the keys, and Melanie slung her purse over her shoulder.

At first, they walked along the road in silent accord, Melanie's hand tucked into Peter's. She breathed deeply of the morning air, not even minding the dust they were stirring up. It was a glorious day, and she was happy simply to be alive. Peter's fingers interlocked more firmly with hers, and he began to swing their arms up and down. Finally he actually broke into song! "I'm a travelin' man, who'll pick any road, s'long as it leads where I wanna go—"

Melanie chuckled. "Peter, speaking of destinations—or should I say, singing of them—do you have any idea where we are?"

He shrugged, continuing to swing their arms. "A considerable distance from Fort Worth. Somewhere in west Texas. I just sort of headed west last night with no particular place in mind."

"So you don't really know the territory?"

He stopped walking abruptly, turning to her in pretended horror and assuming a mock-Texan drawl. "Lady, do you mean to tell me you're a born-and-bred Texan and you don't know your home state any better than I, a virtual newcomer, a man who's been in Fort Worth a mere year and a half?"

Melanie assumed a haughty southern belle accent. "You must remembuh, Petuh deah, that whenevuh ah travel across Texas, ah arrive and depart by chartered flights."

Peter laughed, his husky chuckle echoing into the dusty distance. "Then I guess it's the ignorant leading the ignorant."

"Something like that," Malanie agreed merrily, following the erratic flight of a butterfly with an appreciative eye. "So, as we continue traveling down life's highway, so to speak, why don't you sing me the rest of your little song?"

As they began walking again, Peter burst into another improvised lyric. "I'm a travelin' man, far from home, with no real roots, but happy to roam."

The catchy song sparked Melanie's curiosity. "Where is home, anyway, Peter?"

He sent a large piece of gravel sailing down the road with a sharp kick. "I grew up all over the world. Spent several years living in luxury town houses and hotels until my dad's . . . business failed. I was around twelve when that happened. After that, I was shuffled among various relatives here in the States. None of them had much time or patience to waste on me, so I sort of came up through the school of hard knocks. But I survived. I even put myself through college."

"Why couldn't you stay with your own family after your father's business failed?" Melanie asked, incredulous to learn that Peter had been farmed out for the latter part of his childhood.

His grip on her hand tightened. "Mel, my father is Vance Valentine." When he saw no flicker of recognition in her eyes, he went on. "He was a notorious jewel thief who survived very well for years under a string of aliases. My mother and he were never married. She left when I was about nine. Guess she got tired of sneaking out of places in the dark whenever the police started to close in on Dad. She must have known his luck would eventually run out. And it did, years later. One of my father's accomplices botched a job, and they were all caught and sentenced to lengthy prison terms. My father's still serving time."

Melanie was stunned, not so much by the news that Peter's father was a crook as by Peter's success in spite of his unstable background. She turned to him, noticing the tension beneath his casual pose. Lovingly she ran a hand along his jaw. "I think it's a miracle you turned out to be the kind of person you are today," she said sincerely. "You overcame the worst of odds, Peter. You should be very proud of that."

He reached up and covered her hand with his own. "I don't tell many people that story, Mel, but I wanted you to know. My childhood wasn't easy, but I think it made me stronger in some respects. I didn't have many friends because we moved often, and I was afraid to get close to people for fear they'd figure out exactly who my father was. Later, after he was arrested and the truth came out, kids began to shun me." He laughed softly. "Would *you* invite the son of a thief to your child's birthday party? My few pals were those I met at neighborhood rec centers. Most of them came from unstable homes, too, so I didn't particularly stand out."

Suddenly Melanie felt ashamed of herself. In many ways she and Peter had experienced similar problems growing up. Both of them had felt shut out because of their family circumstances. Neither had made many real friends. But she'd chosen to hide from the world, whereas Peter had met it head on, struggling and moving ahead until he reached the top of his field, in spite of the odds against him. Unlike Melanie, he'd taken chances along the way, and he'd developed into a confident man, who'd learned to consider not only his own needs but also those of others.

"You're remarkable, Peter," she said softly. "You could have become a juvenile delinquent, but instead you're preventing crime. And you haven't withdrawn from life. You've learned how to cope with it."

He bent to brush her lips with his own. "It's easy, Mel," he said tenderly. "You just have to meet one challenge at a time."

She lifted her fingers to her mouth, tracing the outline of his kiss. The briefest contact with him made her happy. But more and more she realized that her feelings for him were based on more than physical attraction. She admired him, respected him, and—wonder of wonders—after the last few hours they'd spent together, she even trusted him.

Somewhere in the distance a robin's early-morning call trilled, piercingly sweet. The sun rose higher in the sky, and the scent of wildflowers floated on the cool breeze. Melanie's heart felt full with the wonder of the day, and with her growing self-confidence. For the first time in a long while, she trusted her instincts to lead her exactly where she wanted to go.

Smiling at Peter, she urged him forward with the gentle

pressure of her fingertips on his arm. "Want to hear a little song of mine?" she asked softly.

"Only if you can carry a tune better than I can," he teased.

She made a face. "Rest easy. You're looking at a former member of Miss Pomeroy's Finishing School Choir." She cleared her throat before beginning to sing in a clear soprano: "I'm a travelin' woman—left it all behind, to hit the road with Valentine."

"Might not make the top forty, but I love the sentiment," he replied huskily.

"Me, too," she agreed, sliding an arm around his waist.

Chapter

8

THREE DUSTY MILES LATER, Peter and Melanie caught their first glimpse of civilization. A roadside café and gas station loomed up beyond a graveled parking area dotted with scraggly weeds. Several pickup trucks were parked outside the café. A couple of them bore bumper stickers that read, "If you ain't country, you ain't cool."

"I'm going to order the tallest glass of orange juice on the menu," Melanie declared as their feet scrunched across the gravel. "The beer I had last night and dust I swallowed today have made me really thirsty. And then maybe I'll have some bacon and eggs, a side order of toast, and a big helping of hash browns."

"Some people think falling in love increases their appetites," Peter remarked as he held open the door of the café.

Did he say "love"? Melanie asked herself. But she couldn't question him in front of the other patrons. Several men in Stetsons and faded jeans sat at the counter joking and laughing. They turned as the door caught in the breeze and slammed shut behind Peter and Melanie, looked them over curiously, then went back to their conversation.

Peter led Melanie to a corner table for two. A henna-haired waitress in a gingham apron and jeans set two glasses of water in front of them. Melanie gulped hers down in one big swallow, then, smiling apologetically at Peter, drank his, too. The waitress frowned. "You gonna order or what?" she demanded impatiently.

"As soon as you bring us more water, two tall glasses of orange juice, and some coffee," Peter said pleasantly. "The lady's very thirsty."

"This ain't no watering hole, mister," the waitress retorted. "We expect our customers to order food." She pointed to two menus wedged into the napkin holder.

Peter grinned up at her. "While we study the menu, could you please bring us our drinks?"

The waitress hesitated, attempted to give Peter a harsh stare, and failed, obviously succumbing to his charm. "Okay. But I'll be back in a minute," she threatened.

"You certainly won her over," Melanie commented as she scanned the handwritten menu Peter handed her.

"It's all in the smile, my dear," he teased. "Now, do you know what you want to eat?"

She gave him her order and excused herself to go to the ladies' room, walking behind the tough-looking men huddled at the counter. She washed her face, combed her tangled hair, and attempted to smooth out the wrinkles in her clothes. Then she applied a little lipstick and powdered her nose.

When she returned to the table, a radio was blaring out country music. She sat down across from Peter, pleased to see that the beverages had already been served. She drank her orange juice, then a cup of coffee, leaned back in her chair, and sighed. "I feel like a new woman," she proclaimed.

"You look marvelous, Mel," Peter complimented her. "I think being kidnapped agrees with you."

She raised a brow. "Shame on you, Peter! As my personal bodyguard, you should have prevented me from being abducted."

He flashed a provocative smile. "Give me some credit, Mel. I allowed only a certain kind of man to kidnap you."

"Mmmm . . . And what kind of man is he?" she teased.

His expression turned serious. "Someone who really cares about you, who believes that he can make you completely happy, and—"

He was interrupted by the arrival of the waitress, who set steaming plates of food in front of them. Hungry though she was, Melanie silently cursed the woman's timing. Had Peter been on the verge of making a declaration?

"That it?" the waitress asked, "or do you want more to drink?" She glared pointedly at Melanie.

"We'll let you know if we need anything else," Peter said. "Thank you."

The waitress shrugged, but managed to send a tiny smile toward him, ignoring his troublesome companion and smacking her order pad against her thigh.

In between bites Melanie said, "Boy! That woman's a real Miss Congeniality."

"I've met a few like her over the years," Peter replied. "She's probably underpaid, overworked, and worrying about how she's going to feed all those hungry mouths at home."

Melanie reflected on his comment for a moment. She'd accused her family of not being in touch with real life, but she was beginning to realize that she didn't know much more about it than they did. She'd never even been inside a place like this before. Her dining experiences had been confined to meals at home or in the sumptuous surroundings of exclusive restaurants, where well-paid and impeccably trained waiters catered to her every request. "Let's leave her a big tip," she said quietly.

The door banged shut, and a youngster entered the café with a stack of newspapers, which he deposited unceremoniously on the counter. "Anybody wanna buy the Sunday edition before I put 'em all in the machine outside?" he asked.

Several of the customers at the counter dug into their pockets and slapped change into the boy's hand. Then the young carrier gathered up the extras and left. Melanie chuckled softly. "I'll bet you'd never see anybody perform that kind of service in the city," she said.

"Probably not," Peter agreed. "But the boy may make a

little extra here and there by being so enterprising. With that kind of attitude he ought to go far in life."

Melanie was struck again by the differences between Peter's perspectives and her own. It had never occurred to her that the boy might be trying to get ahead, not just performing a courtesy. The voice of a newscaster on the radio interrupted Kenny Rogers's mellow tones and her thoughts. "Peter, listen..."

But his attention was already riveted on the radio as the newscaster continued. "The heiress was last seen on Saturday in her family's Fort Worth mansion. It is believed that her personal bodyguard, Peter Valentine, kidnapped the thirty-year-old woman. Worth Carroway, her multimillionaire father, has offered one hundred thousand dollars to anyone who can provide substantial information about his daughter's whereabouts. In addition, a quarter of a million dollars is being offered as a reward for the heiress's safe return. As yet, no ransom demands have been received by the family. Melanie Carroway is five feet six inches tall, with auburn hair and brown eyes. She weighs about one hundred fifteen pounds. If anyone has any knowledge of—"

"Oh, my stars," Melanie whispered. "Peter, I thought you told Brown—"

"I *did* tell him we'd be gone a couple of days, Mel," he returned in a low, agitated voice. "He must have screwed up the message. Damn!"

Melanie leaned across the table, speaking in quietly urgent tones. "We've got to get out of here before these people figure out who we are and call the police. Those men look so mean that I don't dare use the pay phone here, but if we can find somewhere safe, I can call home and explain everything."

Peter patted her hand in reassurance. "Okay, don't panic. The thing to do is act casual. Let's get up, pay our bill, and just leave."

She nodded and gathered up her purse as Peter left a good-sized tip on the table. They were halfway to the cash register when a burly man in a checked shirt let out an excited cry, jabbing his thumb in Melanie's direction. "Hey, Jed, don't she look like the picture in the paper?"

Melanie raised a hand to hide her face. Jed stared at the black-and-white photo his pal was waving in front of him. *"Looks like?* Hell! That's her! She's the Carroway broad!"

The rest of the customers at the counter turned as if in slow motion, their eyes traveling to Melanie's face, then back to the newspaper photo. The waitress slapped her forehead as she glanced quickly at the picture. "Sure, she is! Probably been drugged. That's why she acted so funny. She just kept drinking and drinking—"

"Wait a minute!" Peter began, holding up a warning hand. But it was too late. The men were climbing off their stools and advancing slowly toward them.

"Just come over here, missy," the first man said softly. "I'll protect you from him." He gestured menacingly toward Peter.

Peter moved quickly in front of Melanie. "Back toward the door," he said softly.

She complied immediately, taking small, tentative steps. The burly man's arm shot out at Peter, who ducked, whirled, and brought his leg up in a kick that knocked his assailant backwards into his buddies. The other men toppled like bowling pins as the waitress huddled behind the counter and screamed, "Watch out! He knows that fancy karate stuff. He could have a gun!"

Peter grabbed Melanie's hand and pulled her hurriedly through the door. "What are we going to do?" she cried. "We have no car—"

"Just keep running, Mel." She glanced back over her shoulder and saw him hurl the newspaper vending machine against the café door. In seconds he was at her side again, taking her hand in his. They sprinted across the parking area, gravel flying from beneath their heels. A late-model convertible careened past them, its four young passengers bouncing to the blaring sound of taped rock music. It slowed as it approached the gas station, and Peter lit out in a dead run for the car. As the driver braked to a complete stop by the gas pump, Peter lifted her into the back seat between a couple, who looked up in astonishment as he leapt agilely onto the platform behind the rear seat, his legs wedged on either side of Melanie.

"I'll pay you everything I've got in my pocket if you'll get us away from here!" he yelled.

The driver turned, his mouth open, and stared with disbelief at Melanie and Peter, who pressed a hundred and then a fifty into his hand. "It's all I've got. Drive!" he ordered.

"Please!" Melanie echoed frantically.

The driver's gaze traveled past Peter's shoulders toward the men in the café, who had managed to break down the door and were kicking at the overturned newspaper vending machine.

"There they are!"

"Close in on 'em now!"

"Ain't gonna let that money slip through my fingers!"

"We can all claim a piece of that reward!"

"Her daddy won't even miss them big bucks!"

The sight of the mob advancing toward his car made up the driver's mind. "I don't know what's going on, but I'm sure not sticking around to find out," he shouted, stepping on the accelerator. The convertible shot back onto the road in a cloud of dust.

"What in the hell's going on, mister?" the male half of the couple in the back seat yelled up at Peter. "You didn't rob that café, did you?"

"Absolutely not!" Melanie said, clinging to Peter's ankle.

"Bunch of malcontents in there," Peter explained loudly. "They didn't agree with our politics!"

The girl on Melanie's right leaned forward to tap the shoulder of the driver's date. "Amy, can you believe this? Isn't it exciting? A high-speed getaway—just like in the movies!" Amy turned around with a peculiar green look on her face and buried her head in her hands.

The driver checked his rearview mirror. "Damn!" he cried. "Those guys are *chasing* us!"

Melanie twisted in her seat to see a string of pickup trucks in hot pursuit of the convertible. Several men leaned out the windows, shouting things she couldn't hear over the wind and the throb of the drums on the car's tape deck. Her grip on Peter's ankle tightened.

Suddenly Amy found her voice, speaking in barely controlled tones. "We've been out all night partying, and we just decided to have a picnic in the country today before we returned to TCU. Midterms are coming up, and we just thought we'd have some fun. But this is too much." She shook her head, covering her eyes with her hands as she slumped down in the seat.

Melanie glanced behind them at the same time Peter did. The trucks and their determined drivers were gaining on the convertible! "Open it up!" Peter yelled. "Come on!"

"Mister, I don't know these roads as well as those guys! Besides, they probably all have high-lift cams and four-barrel carburetors on those damned trucks! How the hell do you expect me to outrun them?" He glanced again in the rearview mirror and pressed the accelerator harder. His date screamed as the car picked up speed and Peter wobbled perilously, clenching Melanie's shoulders. The car took a curve at an alarming rate of speed, then careened around a corner.

Melanie shut her eyes until she realized they hadn't rolled over. The girl in the seat next to her glanced over her shoulder. "We've lost them!" she cried excitedly. "I don't think they saw us turn onto this side road!"

"It's only a matter of time before they catch up," her date replied. He leaned forward to talk to the driver. "Listen, Bob, how about dumping these two off? They're the only reason those goons are chasing us."

"Oh, no, you can't," Melanie protested. "Please. Just take us to the next town."

Amy sat up straight and whirled around to fix Melanie with a piercing stare. "You don't know this part of west Texas, do you, lady? There aren't any towns for fifty miles! Besides, you've caused enough trouble." She seized the driver's arm. "Bob, make them get out—now!" Her voice had risen to a shrill whine.

The convertible came to a screeching halt at the side of the road, and four pairs of eyes turned accusingly on Melanie and Peter. "Do you have any cash, Mel?" Peter asked. "I'm cleaned out."

She shook her head. "No, I rarely ever carry any. Just a few credit cards—"

"Get out!" Amy screamed hysterically. "Now! Before

those men show up! We wouldn't take any more money as a bribe even if you had it. Just leave!"

"Amy has a nervous problem," explained the young woman next to Melanie. "She's in psychology."

"I'm not in psychology!" Amy cried. "I mean, I don't go to a psychologist. I'm hoping to become one!"

"Good luck," Peter said brusquely, hopping over the side of the car. He reached in to lift Melanie out and set her carefully on the ground. Amy punched the shoulder of the driver who hesitated briefly before gunning the convertible on down the road, spraying Melanie and Peter with a fine coating of dust.

"Thanks for the lift!" Peter muttered into the distance.

Melanie leaned wearily against him, wiping her grimy face. "Oh, Peter, what are we going to do? We don't have a dime to our names, and we can't risk asking to use someone's phone, even if we find one, because the people might recognize me from the newspaper picture and turn us in!"

Peter drew her into his arms. "We'll think of something, Mel. In the meantime we'd better stay off the roads and travel cross country. I most definitely do not want to meet up with our pals from the café."

As they skirted a draw, a jack rabbit bounded out of the undergrowth, making Melanie jump. "Oh! I'm a little nervous, I guess," she apologized breathlessly.

Peter caught her hand. "Mel, I'm sorry as hell things turned out this way. We're in pretty serious trouble, I'm afraid."

She squeezed his fingers. "Peter, if I'm going to be stranded in the far reaches of Texas, there's no one I'd rather have protecting me than you. Honestly. I trust you."

"You don't know how much it means to me to hear you say that, Mel."

"And you don't know how much it means to me to *believe* it," she answered. "Trust is something I never really had in my marriage. To be truthful, I've never experienced it with any man—until you."

Peter placed a hand on either side of her face, his gaze

reflecting his deep emotion. "I want you, Mel. So very much. You know that, don't you?"

She nodded, trembling slightly, then whispered against his mouth, "This isn't the time or place, but maybe..."

He closed his eyes briefly. "You're right. Let's concentrate on finding somewhere safe first." With obvious reluctance, his jaw clenched tightly, he released her from his embrace, shoved his hands in his pockets, and inhaled deeply. Still trembling, Melanie followed him through the tall grass. They'd just made an unspoken promise to make love, as inevitable as the curtain of darkness that would fall tonight, as sure as the sun would rise in the morning...

During the long afternoon hours, Peter and Melanie alternated walking for thirty minutes over the flat terrain with resting in the shade of an occasional tree. Peter told jokes, and they made up more silly song lyrics. A few times they grew tired and her muscles felt stiff, yet Peter's lighthearted chatter and his insistence that they take frequent breaks helped alleviate her exhaustion and take her mind off their perilous situation.

As the afternoon wore on, they grew quiet, too tired and thirsty to sing and talk, acutely aware of each other and the approaching intimacy of darkness. Melanie slipped her hand into Peter's and allowed him to draw her close to his side. Their eyes met with longing. He brushed a kiss across her temple, then bent to move aside a branch that was blocking their path.

They came to a slight incline on the uneven ground. Melanie, stumbling after Peter, felt her foot slip on the loose rocks and shoot out from under her, landing at an awkward angle. Her soft cry brought Peter immediately to her side.

"Are you all right?" he asked anxiously.

"I think so."

"Here, sit down on this rock and let me take a look at it." He squatted in front of her. With warm, sure fingers he removed her shoe, then pushed up her jeans and gently massaged the injured area, sending shivers up her leg. His touch turned soft and caressing, soothing her tired muscles, trailing tingles of desire past her knee to the sensitive skin of her inner thigh. She gave a little moan.

Their gazes locked in a look of intense longing. Wordlessly he smoothed down her pant leg, slipped her shoe back on, and extended a hand to help her to her feet. "Do you feel better now?" he asked huskily.

"My ankle does," she replied softly, "but the rest of me is aching in some new places."

His mouth hovered close to hers. "I'll be happy to soothe *all* your aches very soon, darling Mel."

The sun was lowering when Peter and Melanie discovered a shed surrounded by bushy clumps of mesquite on one side and yellow-brown grass on another. Behind the ramshackle structure lay a cotton field and directly in front of it, autumn wildflowers waved in the breeze. Some distance away, across the slight roll of the plains, was a farmhouse on the rise of a hill.

Melanie looked at Peter expectantly.

"Not exactly the Grand Hotel, is it?" he asked wryly.

"No," she agreed, "but it's a roof over our heads, and the farmhouse is far enough away so that we shouldn't be seen easily."

He nodded and walked over to examine the rusting padlock on the door. Digging into his pockets, he produced an odd-looking tool. A couple of minutes later, the lock sprang open. "We cat burglars do know a few handy tricks," he teased, opening the door wide for her.

She stepped inside, Peter following and pulling the door closed behind him. Two high, narrow, windows shed yellow light on a jumbled pile of rakes, pitchforks, small carts, and other odds and ends along one side wall. Down the middle hung a rope from which dangled a few old clothes. Brokendown furniture, partially covered by loading pads, was piled at the back.

Peter yanked away several of the pads, exposing a child's rocker with a broken armrest, an old butter churn, a chest of blankets, and a scrubbed pine dresser with a huge gash on top. "These pads will make great mattresses and pillows," he said.

"Hmmm..."

He rolled one of the covers into a bolster. "See?"

"Clever," Melanie agreed distractedly, watching the fading light shadow his unshaven face. One still-bright ray bounced off his hair, turning it to silver-gold. In the dim surroundings, his eyes appeared almost turquoise. Even tired and slightly disheveled, he was the sexiest man she'd ever seen.

"Mel?"

"Yes?"

"Bet you didn't figure on a semiprivate room, huh?" He gestured toward the rope of clothes, which formed a curtain of sorts down the middle of the shed.

"No, I didn't."

"Probably isn't room service, though."

"At least we won't have to tip."

"Good thing, since we don't have a dime between us."

"Right."

"No place to clean up either."

"We did that already, remember?" A while back they had found a stream and splashed water on their hands and faces.

"Oh, yeah. Mel?"

"Yes?"

"Which side of the room do you prefer?" His tone was light, but Melanie detected a hint of husky throb in it.

She lifted her eyes to meet his burning gaze. She knew exactly what he meant. And she had no doubt about her answer.

"I want to sleep with you," she said clearly.

His brilliant smile made her heart turn over. His eyes flickered toward the rope of clothes. "Shall I make the bed near the overalls or that rubber raincoat?"

"It was raining when we first met," she replied softly, "so the rubber raincoat, by all means."

Peter spread three thicknesses of material over the flooring, just to one side of where an olive-green rubber raincoat hung from the rope, then fashioned another pillow and placed it next to the one he'd already made. He bent to fold back the top blanket before straightening and catching her smiling approval. "Our bed wouldn't look better to me if it had silk sheets on it," she murmured.

He took her hand and led her to the bed. Silently they lay down together on their backs with their shoulders and thighs barely touching. He turned toward her. "Melanie, I want you more than I've ever wanted anything in my life." His voice was silky, his breath hot in her ear.

Her own breath fluttered, then caught in her throat. Slowly, she placed her hand on his chest. She could feel the heat emanating from him, the rapid racing of his heart through his sweater and shirt. "I want you, too," she whispered.

"Do you know how long I've waited to hear you say those words? How many nights I've lain awake thinking what making love to you would be like?"

Her reply was muffled by the hard curve of his shoulder as he pulled her to him. She buried her lips in the warm flesh of his neck, threading her fingers through his thick hair. Then, as he lifted his head to gaze down at her, she traced the hollow beneath his cheekbone.

Wordlessly he slid his hands under the waistband of her sweater and tugged it over her head. She smiled. Only with Peter Valentine would it seem perfectly natural to make love in a shed, lying on loading pads with the olive-green rubber raincoat fluttering above them. "I'll never complain about rainy weather again," she whispered.

"I have a thing for raincoats, especially rubber ones," he confessed teasingly. But his tone was filled with underlying currents of desire.

Her thoughts vanished as Peter slipped off her pink jersey top, and his fingers danced fleetingly over the deep cleavage revealed. She shuddered with pleasure as he unhooked the clasp of her lacy bra. Gently, he slid it down her arms and threw it to one side.

She gazed into his eyes, stunned by the reverence with which he was studying her. "You're incredibly beautiful," he gasped, cupping one breast in his hand. He bent to take the hardening nipple into his mouth, and Melanie moaned softly. No one had ever touched her in this gently demanding manner. She was discovering that Peter made love without reservation, giving and receiving the greatest pleasure possible.

Sunbursts went off in her head, blazing brightly behind her half-closed eyes. He lifted his mouth from her breast, then balanced the other one in his palm. He caught the nipple between his tongue and lower lip, stroking the bud until it ripened full-blown. She moaned again and spread her shaking hands beneath his sweater, urging him to help her remove it.

Peter sat up, quickly shedding his sweater and shirt and flinging them aside. In the ephemeral light, his chest gleamed like molten gold. Melanie held out her arms and he lay down beside her again, the full length of their bodies touching. As if they were blind, their hands sought and traveled over each other's bare torsos, moving intimately down their still-clothed hips and thighs.

Deep purple shadows replaced the dying rays of sunlight as Melanie caressed the hard planes of Peter's shoulders, ran her hands down the sides of his rib cage, and explored his firm, trim abdomen. His hand cradled the nape of her neck, urging her lips to his chest. The old Melanie Carroway would have felt self-conscious teasing his flat brown nipples with her tongue, but the new Melanie took delight in pleasing her lover. Her hands caught in the golden chest hair as her mouth probed each nipple. Then Peter's mouth performed the same magic on her before moving down to her narrow midriff, and slowly back up to the pulsating hollow at the base of her throat.

"You're everything I envisioned," he murmured, his voice soft, low, filled with the straining chords of desire. "But I want to see all of you, be part of you . . ."

They sat up, removing the rest of their clothing at the same pace. Then he turned to her once again, slowly laying her back down, cradling the dip of her spine, then fanning his hands over her curving buttocks. Balancing himself above her, he bent to kiss her fully on the mouth. It was like no other kiss they'd ever shared. As his tongue slipped past her lips, wonderful sensations burst forth—the taste and scent of sun-baked sand, autumn flowers, a hint of cologne, and his pure maleness.

Slowly he withdrew his mouth from hers and encircled her waist with his hands. She could feel the hard evidence of his desire thrusting against her thigh, but he remained motionless, looking down into her eyes. He bent closer, smiling slightly, his lids half closed. "Touch me," he pleaded, his tone ragged. "Please."

Her fingers closed gently around him, stroking and caressing until a husky groan tore from his throat. She was stunned by the pleasure she was giving him and herself. And when his fingers carefully probed the inner core of her desire, she lost what little control she had, crying out.

"I want to make sure you're ready for me," he whispered. "I don't want to hurt you, Mel . . ."

"You won't . . . Please, Peter," she begged.

Slowly, gently, he entered her, tentatively pressing his weight down over the soft curves of her body. She arched impatiently against him, fanning her hands along his strong back, clasping him closer to her, feeling the insatiable craving of appetites she'd never known she possessed. She became daring, eager to feel the full, hard length of him inside her. Her hands slid to his buttocks, pressing him farther into her moist depths.

Making love with Peter was like nothing she'd ever known. They moved together perfectly, establishing their own rhythms. Her body ceased to have boundaries; her mind, limits. And then, in a split second of time, she crossed over to another dimension, where she lay suspended, beyond the constraints of any previous physical awareness. They'd reached some distant shore, a beautiful place she didn't want to leave. At Peter's first intimate touch, something inside her had flowered, and now it burst open, fully and completely. Until this moment, she thought wonderingly, she'd been half alive.

They lay motionless for some time, breathing deeply, taking in the dewy scent of their moist bodies. At last, Peter rolled slowly to his side, balanced himself on an elbow, and looked down at her with a piercingly bright gaze. "I can still feel myself inside you, Mel," he whispered. "You're the most beautiful thing that's ever happened to me. But I knew it would be like this almost from the moment I first saw you—seconds after you discovered me in the library that dark, rainy night..."

Melanie lay as if weightless, suspended in her own happiness. Why had it taken her so long to trust Peter? she wondered. But she knew the answer: Her own refusal to taste life to the fullest had forced her to hold back that trust. Only after he made her see the world through different eyes had she let go of her old fears and prejudices. He had helped her redefine herself and her needs. He'd encouraged her to emerge from the cocoon she'd deliberately spun about herself, made her discover the best parts of life. Now she could meet each day as a fresh challenge, with courage to go after what she truly wanted, no longer afraid to be herself. She wasn't so naive as to expect her transformation to be *complete* so soon, but she was proud that she'd come so far. How had she ever thought she could be satisfied with standing on the outside looking in?

"Thank you, Peter, for making these the happiest days in my life," she whispered as a tear trickled down her cheek. Gently, he brushed it away, smiling in unspoken understanding.

Then he drew her against him and pulled the blanket over their naked bodies. Just before her heavy lids closed, she saw through the window that the moon had come out, its pale rays casting them in silver as it moved slowly across the Texas sky.

Chapter

9

MELANIE STIRRED, OPENED her eyes, and flung an arm over her face to block the bright sunshine streaming through the windows. "Mmmph," she muttered, rolling over to press closer to the warm body lying next to her. Half consciously she rubbed her chin against hard back muscles, then groggily fit herself into the curve of a spine. Ah, that felt wonderful. Like a warm nest she never wanted to leave.

"Mel . . ." Peter's voice was still husky from sleep.

"Hmmm . . ."

"Honey, if you keep this up, we're never going to get out of this shed."

"Mmmm . . ." She snuggled still closer, hovering between consciousness and sleep, as Peter rolled over to face her.

A leg moved over her hip. A toe wriggled sensuously up her calf. "Come on, Mel, we need to get moving before somebody finds us here."

"Feels good," she mumbled as the toe continued to lightly caress her leg, then the sensitive spot behind her knee.

"Yeah?" He sat up suddenly, jerking most of the covers with him. "Well, if you like that so much, how about this?" Before she knew what was happening, he'd knelt at the end of the bed and begun to tickle her toes.

"Oh, Peter! Stop! Please!" Melanie struggled to seize his nimble fingers, but he was too quick for her.

"Peter!" she cried, gasping for breath between fits of laughter.

"Are you going to wake up and get dressed?" he demanded.

She nodded, attempting to yank her feet away from him.

"Can't hear you, Mel."

"Yes!" she shouted.

"Promise?"

"Oh! Yes! Yes! Yes!"

The tickling ceased. Melanie blinked away tears of laughter, gradually focusing on Peter's face. "You're more persistent than an alarm clock," she complained.

"I think we ought to get on the move again before—" He frowned. Melanie had begun to trace a pattern with her toes along his chest.

"Doesn't that feel good, Peter?" she asked innocently.

"Yeah, sure. But, honey, we should get dressed and try to call your family before this situation gets any more out of hand."

"*I'm* already out of hand, I'm afraid," she whispered suggestively as she reached for his hand.

He feigned shock, lifting both brows, but his expression changed abruptly when Melanie dragged him toward her. "Lie back down," she pleaded. "Here, next to me."

"Mel," Peter groaned, even as he complied with her request, "this is the most brazen display of—"

She smiled seductively, balanced herself on an elbow, and bent to cover his face with quick kisses. Pausing momentarily between his nose and upper lip, she asked, "Brazen display of what, Peter, hmmm?"

One hand lifted to caress her face. "The most brazen display of lust I've ever witnessed."

She chuckled, pressing her mouth to his ear. "Have you had a lot of experience . . . with lust?"

His breathing became heavier. "Not as much as I'd like."

She swatted his chest playfully. "In the future, you are to—Oh!" Peter's fingers were skimming her inner thigh, barely touching her skin. She shivered. "Oh! You are to take out your lustful impulses only on me," she gasped. "No one else. Understood?"

"Perfectly, Mel," he returned unevenly as she nibbled at a sensitive place between his shoulder and neck. "Mmmm ...It's taken me much too long to find you, the real you, the woman I always knew you were deep down. Do you honestly think I'd even"—Melanie gently bit his earlobe— "look at another woman?" he finished raggedly, raining kisses from her forehead to the tip of her nose.

He continued on to her chin, then began to kiss the column of her throat. She moaned softly. "Peter..."

"Hmmm?" He seemed totally absorbed in tasting every inch of her shoulder.

"Have there been lots of other women in your life?"

His head lifted. "One- hundred- and- fifty-two, to be exact."

She chuckled. "Did any of them like rubber raincoats?"

He sighed. "No. And that, frankly, was what always came between us. You're the only one I could find who shared my penchant for"—his eyes drifted up to the raincoat hanging above them—"olive green rubber," he finished dryly.

Melanie ran her fingers over the golden stubble of his beard. "Remember that I like anchovies, too," she said softly.

He sat up, bending over her. "You're a very special woman, Mel."

"Because I like rubber raincoats and anchovies?" she asked tremulously, looking into his beautiful eyes.

"Partly. But mostly because you're you." His expression was no longer teasing.

Her heart sang for joy even as she wondered how he could have known she was capable of changing from a tightly closed bud to a fully flowered blossom. How had he ever had the patience to await her transformation? What had made him know that she was special from the very first?

"Do you remember my asking you when we first met if you believed in karma, Mel?" he asked.

She nodded, smiling. "Yes."

"Well, I don't know if there really is such a thing. All I know is that for most of my life I've been guided by powerful instincts that have usually led me in the right direction." His voice was huskier than usual as he continued, "I can't explain how I knew you were what I'd been searching for. I just did. Shortly after you walked into the library, everything that had been missing from my life was suddenly present—there in the room with us, too powerful to be ignored."

Melanie took his face in her hands. "Oh, Peter, I felt all of that, too. I just wouldn't allow myself to hope, so I hid my true feelings, as I've done for so long, tellling myself you were just like Rip. I was afraid of suffering more pain, afraid to believe you had all of Rip's best qualities and none of the bad."

Peter gathered her to him, embracing her with strong yet infinitely gentle hands as he covered her mouth in a long, sweetly demanding kiss. They drew apart slowly, gazing into each other's eyes, silently communicating an emotion that needed no words.

Then, without warning, the moment was shattered by a loud voice that sounded as if it were coming over a public address system. "This is Captain Walters of the Texas Rangers. We have you surrounded. Release the hostage at once and come out slowly with your hands over your head."

Melanie's face turned ashen. "Oh, Peter! They've found us! How—?"

He muttered a string of oaths, and jumped to his feet.

"Honey," he began evenly, scrambling for his clothes, "the first thing to do is get dressed. I'll go outside and explain—"

"No! Peter, they might shoot you!"

"Mel, they're not going to shoot me if I just walk out of the shed with my hands over my head and talk to them calmly."

"No, Peter," she countered firmly. "I'll go out first and talk to them so there'll be absolutely no misunderstanding about my being kidnapped."

"Mel, I'm not going to allow—"

"If you don't, I'll follow you through that door stark naked," she returned sweetly.

He reflected on this possibility for a moment, then met her determined eyes. "You win," he said quietly.

The Ranger's voice barked out another warning. "You have three minutes!"

Melanie's fingers shook as she pulled on her clothes and ran trembling hands through her hair. "I'm ready," she announced with more conviction than she felt.

Peter, too, was fully dressed by now. "Mel, let me go out first."

She kissed him quickly on the mouth. "After I talk to them, when I think it's perfectly safe, you may come out. They're not going to do anything to me, Peter, because they believe I'm the victim."

Before he could protest further, she pushed open the door of the shed and slipped outside. At first, she had trouble adjusting to the bright glare of the early-morning sun, but as she walked hesitantly forward, she was aware of low voices coming from everywhere around her.

She raised a hand to her forehead to shield her eyes and saw quite clearly that she was surrounded by an army of Texas Rangers! They were crouched behind clumps of mesquite, kneeling behind cars, even lying flat on their stomachs in the grassy plain. Each wore a white Stetson, the five-point stars of their shiny silver badges shone blindingly brilliant in the sun, and they all looked deadly serious. But most frightening of all was that every single man held a shotgun pointed directly at her!

Captain Walters, it turned out, was a quietly determined man. He had not earned a coveted position in the elite corps of the Texas Rangers by being a pushover or taking his job lightly. Melanie finally managed to explain the misunderstanding involved in the purported kidnapping. But first she had to back against the shed door and refuse to budge until the Rangers listened to her story! Even then, Captain Walters's only concession was to give Peter a chance to come out on his own free will instead of forcing him out with teargas! The minute he emerged from the shed, Melanie attempted to rush to his side, but the Rangers held her back. Her "abductor" was frisked, clapped in handcuffs, and whisked into a police car.

She tried to reason with the Rangers, but Captain Walters remained unconvinced, repeatedly telling her he was following correct procedure and that if her story was true, not merely a fabrication invented because she was experiencing stress sympathy for her abductor, everything would be settled satisfactorily in time. Meanwhile, she was to ride in his car with him.

Slumped in the seat, Melanie asked him how he and his men had found her and Peter. He pushed his Stetson back on his graying head, the laugh lines around his mouth crinkling slightly. "Farmer up the road went to his shed to get some tools early this morning, noticed the padlock had been tampered with."

"That's all?" Melanie cried incredulously.

Captain Walters cleared his throat. "He—uh—had a ladder propped up in back of the shed, so he dragged it around, climbed up on it, and peered into a window. Said he couldn't make out much because the panes were cloudy and the sun wasn't all the way up, but he could see a man and a woman sleeping together inside. He'd read about this case, so he called us immediately."

Once, Melanie would have turned crimson at this report, but now she merely cursed the farmer's efficiency in getting an early start on the day. Besides, she and Peter had been covered with blankets, so the farmer couldn't have seen anything but their heads. "Well, Captain," she said, smiling, "that should be proof enough that I was in the shed of my own choosing. Why else would I have been sleeping with a man who's supposed to have abducted me?"

"He could have had you restrained in some way, Miss Carroway," Captain Walters replied calmly. "Even kidnappers need to sleep occasionally."

Melanie sighed. For people in real trouble, she was glad the Texas Rangers took their job so seriously, but in this instance, she wished Captain Walters would forget bureaucratic procedure. There was nothing she could do, however, except wait until they arrived back home. She smiled. Only her father could have talked the Texas Rangers into driving them directly to the mansion instead of to regional headquarters. The very private Worth Carroway, with millions of dollars at his disposal, must have used all of his clout to arrange a low-key homecoming. Melanie was particularly grateful because of the nagging conviction that if they were going anywhere near a jail Peter would be summarily thrown behind bars.

That afternoon, the procession of Texas Ranger vehicles drove through the massive wrought-iron gates of the Carroway mansion past a group of shouting reporters. The newsmen's voices became even louder as the gates closed behind the Rangers, prohibiting the reporters from entering the grounds. As the captain's car rounded the bend, Melanie saw her father, Aunt Maddie, McNurty, Brown, and even Harris awaiting their arrival. The car had barely halted when she jumped out, intent on running toward the car in which Peter was riding, but the good captain caught her gently by the arm. "Not until we have everything straightened out, Miss Carroway."

Cameras clicked, and the excited members of the press pushed against the gates until Captain Walters held up a warning hand.

Resignedly, Melanie allowed him to escort her toward the outstretched arms of her father. "Lamb!" he cried, enfolding her in his embrace. "I've been out of my mind with worry! Are you all right?"

She kissed him on the cheek and her aunt chimed in, "Darling, we didn't know what to do! I just couldn't believe that nice Mr. Valentino would kidnap you, but Harris insisted . . ."

Melanie turned to Harris, who stood to one side, smiling expectantly. "What?" she asked. "Insisted *what?*"

"That you'd been kidnapped, of course," Aunt Maddie said. "Brown gave us a message yesterday. Said Mr. Valentino had told him something or other about your departure." She sighed. "But I think Brown had taken too much medicine again, and his story didn't make a lot of sense. Well, we still weren't too concerned until Harris showed up and we mentioned all of this to him. He demanded we call the authorities at once."

Harris stepped forward, skirting McNurty with obvious distaste. "Dear," he began firmly, "you know how lax your family can be, and I didn't want any more time to pass before the proper people were notified of your disappearance."

Melanie leveled a look of pure disgust on him, starting at the top of his carefully brushed hair and moving down to the shiny toes of his wingtips. "I might have known," she said coldly, "that you were ultimately responsible for this ridiculous mix-up, Harris. You always assume the worst, especially when it comes to my family and me."

His neck grew red, and he cleared his throat loudly. "I'm deeply insulted by your ingratitude, Melanie. That security person kidnapped you, worried us all sick and you're lashing out at *me*." He frowned, flicking a minute piece of lint from his shoulder. "You must be in shock, darling. Why don't you go inside and lie down before you have one of those awful headaches?"

Melanie ignored him, turning back to her father. "Peter did not kidnap me," she said clearly. "In fact, Father, I'm better than I've ever been in my whole life. Peter and I just went on a little trip. He told Brown we'd be gone all weekend, but apparently the message lost something in the translation." She arched a brow at the butler.

Brown drew himself up to his full height, sniffing in outrage. "It's not my fault I began to feel poorly soon after Mr. Valentine told me"—he paused, then concluded vaguely—"whatever it was. At any rate, Melanie, *you're* the one who's besmirched the family name."

Aunt Maddie laid a hand on her arm. "Darling," she began loudly, "I do hope that wherever you and Mr. Valentino stayed, you arranged for separate accommodations." She frowned. "But from your disheveled appearance, I can't imagine what kind of place it must have been. Certainly not one of the finer hotels." Beyond the gates, the reporters scribbled furiously. Melanie could just imagine the field day they'd have with her aunt's pointed comments. As if to punctuate them, McNurty barked loudly.

Worth Carroway regarded her searchingly for a moment, then laid a hand on Captain Walters's shoulder. "I'd like to have a word with you, sir, if I may," he requested. The two men walked a few steps away, their heads bent in earnest conversation. Melanie looked longingly toward the last car, then glared at Harris.

Within minutes, her father and the Ranger rejoined the group. "Melanie, darling," her father began gravely, "are you quite certain that we have misinterpreted this incident?"

"Yes," she answered firmly, "and I know you realize that now, too, Father."

He smiled in agreement. "Indeed. I'm afraid we allowed ourselves to overreact, Captain, as I just explained to you. Actually, my daughter is the only one in the family with perfectly good sense, and I should have relied on that to begin with, instead of being unduly influenced by . . . circumstances."

Melanie hugged her father. "Please ask them to release Peter now," she pleaded.

Captain Walters raised a questioning brow at Worth, who nodded sharply. "Please comply with my daughter's request, Captain. Again, I apologize for the inconvenience, and I'll be glad to meet with you tomorrow to tie up any loose ends. But for now, I'm simply delighted to have my daughter and Mr. Valentine home. I shall accept complete responsibility for Mr. Valentine's release."

The captain hesitated briefly, then signaled to one of his men, who walked briskly down the drive, helped Peter from the car, and removed his handcuffs. Melanie rushed to his side. The reporters' clamor grew louder as they aimed their long-distance lenses, but she and Peter were oblivious of them, lost in the joy of their reunion. "Oh, Peter, are you all right?"

He smiled broadly, assuming his characteristic pose of casual ease. "I'm fine, Mel, as long as you are."

Harris strode angrily forward. "Melanie! Perhaps we were wrong about your being kidnapped, but I do think Mr. Valentine's caused us all enough trouble. I insist that you dismiss him at once. If you do so, I shall be perfectly willing to forgive your disgraceful behavior."

"Back off, will you, Harris, old pal?" Peter said pleasantly, rubbing his wrists where the handcuffs had been.

"I most certainly will not. You can't intimidate me any longer," Harris added bravely, looking meaningfully at the Texas Rangers. "Now, Melanie, go ahead and dismiss Valentine." The reporters, cautiously eyeing the stern-faced Rangers, surged harder against the gates, eager not to miss a word of what had all the potential of becoming a juicy scandal.

Melanie glanced from one man to the other. Despite his perfect grooming and expensive suit, Harris looked shabby in comparison. The younger man had just been through a tough ordeal, but he was smiling his usual confident, in-charge smile. Harris, on the other hand, seemed on the verge of apoplexy over Melanie's refusal to obey his command. His chin trembled dangerously, and his cheeks were puffed out ominously.

Melanie took Peter's arm. "Harris, you are in no position to give me orders—now or in the future. Whatever we had between us is finished. Over. From now on, please don't visit us unless you've been formally invited."

Slack-jawed and speechless, Harris stared at her. So did her father, Aunt Maddie, and Brown. Even McNurty's ears pricked up. Pleased with herself, Melanie struggled to keep from smiling. Her uncharacteristically assertive behavior, coupled with her bizarre conduct over the weekend, had her family and Harris regarding her as if she were an alien being.

It was Brown who found his voice first. "I suggest we go inside and have a drink to celebrate Mr. Mortimer's expedient departure," he mumbled, stumbling through the front door.

By midafternoon, the reporters still hadn't given up. Since the Texas Rangers had departed, they'd even felt free

to shout into an intercom, demanding to be allowed onto
the grounds to interview Melanie. The only thing keeping
them from scaling the fence, Melanie figured, was the fact
that it had electrified wires running along the top. The guard
dogs remained in their run, barking nonstop in response to
all the uproar. The more noise they made, the more McNurty
sulked in a corner, so that even Aunt Maddie was unable
to cajole him back into his usual happy mood.

Somehow, in the midst of the confusion, Peter and Melanie managed to shower, change their clothes, and join the
family in the kitchen. Peter had stationed an employee at
the surveillance monitors in the basement. Any reporters or
overly zealous sightseers who attempted to intrude would
be immediately intercepted.

"I do wish McNurty would join us for some of this
delicious sandwich spread that Cook made," Aunt Maddie
said wistfully, as she, Worth, Brown, Melanie, and Peter
sat at the kitchen table. "He's being so contrary. It think it's
because he doesn't understand what all of the fuss is about."

Picking up on the curiosity behind her aunt's comment,
Melanie realized her family was dying to hear the details
of her weekend. Glancing at Peter, she read his agreement
as clearly as he'd obviously read her mind. Taking turns,
they spent the next half-hour relating the most delightful
aspects of their trip, carefully forgetting to mention that
Peter had planned to "kidnap" her . . . and neglecting to describe their sleeping arrangements in the shed.

As they finished their story, Melanie's father chuckled
and Aunt Maddie clapped her hands. "Oh, it all sounds so
romantic, so daring," she cried. "I can just imagine Harold
sweeping me away for that kind of weekend. He always
loved adventure, you know. The more excitement the better
he liked it—not at all like the present McNurty." She shook
her head ruefully. "He seems to have lost his *joie de vivre*
during his current reincarnation."

"Maybe next time it'll show up again," Peter suggested.

Worth spoke up proudly. "I, for one, Melanie, am glad
you and Mr. Valentine had such a marvelous time together
and that everything turned out well. I'm particularly thrilled

about your success at the art gallery. It gives me hope that I may someday place my novel with a publisher. But, most of all, I'm gratified to see you taking—uh—better charge of your life . . . in some areas."

Melanie chuckled. "More specifically, that translates into getting rid of Harris, doesn't it, Father?"

"Frankly, yes, dear. The man's a bit of a bore."

"I never cared for Mr. Mortimer," Brown stated flatly. "He's entirely too uppity. If Melanie must engage in a dalliance, I much prefer that she do so with Mr. Valentine."

She and Peter exchanged amused glances.

Just then a loud voice bellowed through the intercom again. "We're not leaving until Miss Carroway agrees to an interview!"

"Oh, dear," Aunt Maddie said. "Do you think we're being rude by refusing to talk with them, Mr. Valentino?"

Peter shook his head. "No. In fact, I'd call the police except that those reporters would just return again after the authorities left. Anyway, I've got my man monitoring the grounds, and I'm going to recheck the alarm system myself—just to make sure we keep on top of things."

He rose from the table, smiling at Melanie, although his "See you later" was directed to everyone.

As soon as he disappeared into the basement, Aunt Maddie wandered over to look out the kitchen window. "Goodness," she said, "there are so many of those press people outside the fence. Do you suppose they're thirsty or hungry?"

"Aunt Maddie—" Melanie began, but the little woman was already moving toward the pantry and calling for Cook. Melanie turned a pleading glance at her father. "Aunt's got that look in her eye, Father. I'm afraid she plans to feed all those reporters."

"Hospitality is a mark of good breeding, Melanie," he interrupted. "Surely Mr. Valentine wouldn't object to our serving refreshments. We don't have to let the reporters into the house. They can remain on the other side of the gate. Brown can help Cook pass things through."

The butler shook his head. "Not a chance. My arthritis

is acting up again. No doubt from all the stress." He pushed back his chair and made a great show of hobbling from the kitchen.

"Poor man," Worth said, rising to go into the pantry.

Melanie raced downstairs to tell Peter what her father and aunt were up to. She found Jim, his employee, alone in the control room. Peter had gone to check the window alarms. Melanie found him in the west tunnel several minutes later and had just explained the problem when they heard Jim shout, "Security's been breached!" The sound of stampeding feet and loud voices could be heard clearly.

"Stay on the monitors!" Peter ordered. "I'll see what's going on." He raced up the stairs, Melanie hard on his heels. Glancing over his shoulder, he yelled, "Honey, it might be safer if you'd stay downstairs—"

At that moment, the basement door flew open. Peter and Melanie gasped in unison as they were greeted by a horde of reporters who were munching sandwiches and scribbling on notepads. Aunt Maddie and Worth were pouring drinks, and a sullen-faced Cook stood at the counter preparing more food. The minute Melanie emerged from the basement, the reporters began firing questions at her.

Nearly two hours later, she finally ushered the last reporter out of the library. She'd spent most of the time answering questions she felt were in acceptable taste and sidestepping the others. Actually the interviews had been fun. She had felt confident and poised, and pleased to share her happiness with the world. Her only real concern was for Peter, who, from the moment they'd discovered the press in the kitchen, had been kept busy evicting them from private areas and helping Jim keep track of activity outside. He was worried that some enterprising criminal might take advantage of the chaos by sneaking in and stealing some of the family treasures.

To Peter's credit, he didn't chastise Aunt Maddie or Worth for allowing the reporters to cajole them into opening the gates, although Melanie figured her family probably deserved a good dressing-down. Peter simply quietly and ef-

ficiently dealt with each new problem as it arose, asking
Melanie on several occasions if she really wanted to grant
interviews, explaining she was under no obligation. She
told him she understood, but she felt perfectly capable of
handling the press. After that, he insisted that no more than
six reporters enter the library at a time and not until after
he'd done a security check on them. Then he'd left to attend
to other things.

Melanie was on her way to find Peter when he walked
into the library. She rushed into his arms. "I apologize for
my family, Peter, but you know how naive they are. They
were just outmaneuvered by people who are more savvy."

He stroked her hair, holding her close. "I know, Mel.
Their innocence is partly what makes them appealing, but
those reporters really took advantage of that innocence." He
lifted her chin and gazed down at her. "Do you believe I
actually rousted one guy from your bedroom? He wanted
to take pictures of where you slept!"

Melanie shook her head incredulously. "My bed is for
your eyes only, Peter," she said in a sexy voice.

His hand slid up beneath her breast. "Good. I feel
very possessive about you, Mel. The thought of anyone
encroaching on your private space makes me mad as
hell."

She ruffled her hair. "Is that the green-eyed monster
talking, Peter, or you?"

"Both," he answered huskily, just before he kissed her.

That evening before dinner the entire family gathered in
the library. Melanie watched Peter play checkers with Aunt
Maddie, who was obviously delighted to have found a part-
ner for her favorite game. The other family members always
made excuses to get out of playing with her because she
cheated so flagrantly, which she rationalized by saying she
had been taught different rules. Her manipulations didn't
seem to perturb Peter at all. He accepted them as he did
everything else about the household—with calm equanim-
ity. Every once in a while, he looked up to catch Melanie's
eye, smiling tantalizingly. She returned the attention, en-

joying their silent communication. Maybe tonight after
everyone had gone to bed . . .

Just then, the phone rang. Worth looked up from his
newspaper. "Bother! That confounded instrument hardly ever
rings. Who on earth can it be?"

Brown, aimlessly stirring ice cubes in his drink, paid no
attention.

"Brown, could you please answer the phone?" Melanie
asked.

"Not right now," he returned breezily. "It isn't for me
anyway, and I'm busy."

Melanie was in such a good mood, she merely nodded
and rose to answer the phone herself. Two minutes into the
conversation, she began to smile. "Oh, sure. Yes, we did
have quite a weekend! Next Saturday? That sounds great,
Jody. I'd love it. Yes, I'll tell Peter he can come along."
She laughed mischievously. "Okay, see you then."

As she started to tell Peter about Jody's call, the phone
rang again. This time the caller was the young man she'd
met at the bar who dabbled in art when he wasn't selling
insurance. "Yes, it was a wild time," she agreed. "What a
great idea! I think the kids would love to have more murals
on the walls of the rec center. Yes, I'd love to help you
paint them. Bye."

Again the phone began ringing almost as soon as she
replaced it in the cradle. When she heard Alfred VanZandt's
voice, she clutched the receiver tightly. "What? *You did?*
Already? Oh, my goodness, that's the best news I've had
all day! I just don't know how to thank you, Mr. VanZandt.
Yes, I'll start working on something else right away. Certainly, you have first priority. Oh, I'm so excited! Thank
you so much!"

She executed a little spin, her face glowing. She couldn't
wait to tell Peter! But the second she opened her mouth,
the phone rang yet again. "Hello. Who? Oh, yes, I remember
you, Markham. What prompted you to call me after all
these years?"

Peter rose from the table, a scowl on his face, and came
to stand next to her. Melanie placed her hand over the

receiver. "Just a minute, Peter."

She turned her attention back to her phone conversation. "Well, yes, Markham," she replied, "I suppose I have changed a great deal since our undergraduate days. More adventuresome, yes."

Out of the corner of her eye she saw Peter walk toward the door. She put out a hand to detain him, but he brushed on past her. Frowning, she continued to listen impatiently to her caller. Growing more and more irritated, she finally said firmly, "No, I won't go out with you, Markham. I'm committed to someone else, and anyway, you sound just as insolent and egotistical as ever!" With that, she slammed down the receiver.

Aunt Maddie and her father looked expectantly at her. Brown plunked another ice cube into his drink. "Markham Macy?" Worth asked curiously. "The chap you knew in college? Family's in oil, aren't they?"

She nodded absently, wondering why Peter had left so abruptly. Maybe he needed to check the monitors now that he'd sent Jim back to the agency. "Yes, that's right. Years ago, his path and mine crossed at some function or another. He ran with a wild crowd in those days. Anyway, the evening ended with his telling me that if I ever decided to loosen up, I should call him." She rolled her eyes. "Believe me, he'd be the last man I'd call. He's arrogant, demanding, selfish, which I—"

"Made perfectly clear to him," Worth finished. "Good for you."

Melanie made a sound of disgust. "I might have known he'd crawl out from under his rock once he heard my name in the news. That's just like him—wanting to share the spotlight."

"I'm glad you haven't lost your sense of judgment about what kinds of people are worth your time and affection, dear," Aunt Maddie said proudly.

"If anything, I've developed an even keener sense about what matters to me, Aunt. Listen, did Peter say where he was going?"

Aunt Maddie had lapsed back into her own vague world.

"Ah, let's see . . . I jumped his last man and that was the end of the game. Oh, I think he was going to do some work, maybe."

"Thanks," Melanie said. "I have a lot of good news to share with him, so please excuse me. I'll see you all at dinner."

She headed for the basement, but, to her surprise, found Peter sitting at the kitchen table, staring straight ahead as he sipped from a steaming cup. "Hi. I thought you were working," she began. "Aunt Maddie said—"

"I don't need to work any more tonight," he said. "The system worked perfectly today. Those reporters got inside only because your aunt and father opened the gate for them. Human error is hard to predict."

Melanie frowned. Peter's tone was brusque, tightly controlled; he was obviously holding back his emotions, as if she were a mere client. Something was very wrong.

She walked over to sit down beside him, reaching for his hand. But at that moment he picked up his cup, and her fingers met only the polished surface of the table. "I—I wanted to tell you about all of the phone calls," she began uncertainly.

"You don't owe me that, Mel."

"Owe you?" she echoed, puzzled. "Well, no, Peter, but I'd like to share with you."

He shrugged, his shoulders rising and falling tensely. "I got the gist of all those calls, Mel. Let's see. Jody thinks it would be fun to get together again—you can even bring me! Then my insurance friend asked you to work with him on a mural for the rec center. VanZandt has already sold your paintings and is promising you a very bright career as an artist. He wants you to get busy on something new. And"— he paused, taking a deep breath—"some guy named Markham has decided you're a very exciting woman—which you, of course, encouraged him to think." The pulse at his temple throbbed ominously. "After all, what better way to fan an old flame?"

Melanie gasped. "Peter, do you actually think—"

He rose quickly from his chair and stared coldly down

at her. "What I *think,* Mel, is probably irrelevant. What I *know* is that you're suddenly becoming a very busy woman. Too busy to waste your time talking to me." He turned and left the room without looking back.

Peter didn't join the family for dinner. Melanie fled to her room as soon as the meal was over and sat on the window seat in the darkness, staring out into the star-dotted night. A few hours ago she'd been ecstatically happy. Now she felt as if someone had stolen her key to paradise and trampled it into the dirt. What had come over Peter?

Had she misjudged him after all? Had her sexual surrender been his only goal? Now that he'd had her, was the thrill gone for him?

But as quickly as such thoughts entered her head, she dismissed them. The time they'd spent together this weekend had been truly special. The feelings they shared were mutual. She knew that fact deep inside, clear to the marrow of her bones.

She hadn't given her trust to Peter overnight; she'd slowly but surely bestowed it on him because he deserved it. Even if he hadn't "kidnapped" her, she would have ultimately put her faith in him because he was . . . simply Peter, the man she loved.

Though her instincts told her now that she wasn't wrong about Peter, they also told her that something was very wrong between them.

She sat for a few moments longer, wondering what to do. Then a movement on the lawn below her caught her attention. She peered intently through the windowpane. The subdued lighting on the terrace caught the gleam of Peter's hair as he paced back and forth.

On impulse, Melanie slipped a deep purple shawl over her thin silk dress, hurried downstairs to the wine cellar, found a bottle of champagne, and seized a corkscrew and two crystal glasses from the pantry. She approached the flagstoned terrace quietly, easing out through the parlor door and tiptoeing toward the wrought-iron table, where she placed the champagne and glasses.

Peter stood with his back to her a few yards away, gazing up at the pale moon through the lacy network of dark branches. A gentle breeze caught her skirt, rustling its shimmery lavender folds as she set the corkscrew on the table. At the sound he turned to face her, his features guarded.

"Hi," she said softly, taking a few tentative steps forward.

He was wearing a pale yellow sweater and cream-colored flannel slacks. In the moonlight, his hair appeared silver, a startling contrast to his darkly tanned face. The subtle sheen of his pastel clothing and blond hair was mesmerizing in the evening's hazy incandescence. He walked slowly toward her, an almost larger-than-life figure silhouetted against a backdrop of blue-black sky and the moon's pearly glow. "I've been wanting to talk to you," he said quietly. "I just needed to do something first."

"What's wrong, Peter?" she asked desperately, searching his troubled face.

He jammed his hands into his pockets, then reached out to touch her cheek. "I like to be up front, Mel. Always, if possible." His hand dropped suddenly from her face, and he moved away. "Champagne?" he asked in surprise as his eyes settled on the bottle and glasses.

"I was hoping to seduce you with it," Melanie confessed, coming to stand beside him.

He looked out from beneath his brows. "Is this the same Melanie Carroway who resisted me every inch of the way when we first met?"

"No, it's not. *I'm* not," she corrected. "I've changed because of you, Peter," she added honestly.

"That's what I need to discuss with you, Mel. Changes . . ." He expelled his breath and seemed to make a considerable effort to drag his gaze from the curves of her breasts beneath the light wool shawl. "You've made a lot of changes lately. In fact, you have a whole new life opening up before you. It's become more and more apparent to me that you need to *live* it before you tie yourself down."

Could this be the same persistent, always-sure-of-himself Peter Valentine she knew? She placed a hand on his chest. Even through his sweater, she could feel the rapid thumping

of his heart. He was upset, she realized, *and* aroused by
their physical proximity. Her own heart was beating wildly
for the same reasons.

"When you speak of tying myself down, you're referring
to *our* relationship, is that right, Peter?" she asked carefully,
not certain whether to be angry or frightened.

He looked away, then turned back to her, his eyes a hard
blue glint in the moonlight. "Yes. You see, Mel, in my
eagerness to show you what it meant to follow your heart,
to enjoy life, to take a chance on . . . love, I forgot something
very important."

Melanie's stomach turned over. Suddenly she was terrified. There was no doubt about it now. She clasped her
hands at her waist, desperately trying to compose herself.
"Let me guess," she began lightly, aware that she was trembling. "You have a wife in Peoria."

Peter didn't laugh. He raked a hand through his hair, and
when he spoke, his tone held no amusement. "Mel, you've
fallen in love with life, not with me. I had a hint of it when
you insisted on granting interviews, and I realized it clearly
during your phone conversations. Celebrity status for you
as a person, not simply for your family's wealth, is too
appealing for you to resist. I really came to grips with the
problem when that guy out of your past called and you were
so obsessed with proving to him that you have, indeed,
become a fun-loving, self-possessed woman. You're like a
blind person, Mel, who's able to see for the first time. I
was only the instrument that made possible the wonderful
sensations you're experiencing.

"It wouldn't be fair to me or to you to continue our
relationship right now," he went on. "You need time to enjoy
yourself, to put your priorities in order. Maybe later on, I
can . . . assume a place in your life."

Melanie stared at him in speechless horror. If she'd appeared enthralled by the sights and sounds of her new world,
it was only because she was in love with Peter, not because
she wanted to break hearts and engage in late-night reveling.
Why couldn't he believe that?

The loosely knotted shawl slipped off her left shoulder,

revealing the deep plunge of her neckline. She realized she was fighting for her life now, and the fear she'd felt at first was suddenly replaced by anger. "Who appointed you judge and jury, Peter?" she demanded. "Have you ever considered that perhaps you haven't interpreted things correctly? That just maybe your amazing perceptive powers have failed you this one time? That perhaps I don't care to live my life without you?" Her voice broke. "That I . . . love you?"

He caught her suddenly around the waist with one strong arm. "I wish I could believe you, Mel. Eventually, maybe it'll be true. I know you think it's true now, but you're still riding the carousel, in love with love. For the first time, you're pleasing yourself completely, and that's wonderful. But it doesn't mean you love me. Not yet . . ." His voice held a note of finality as he added, "I'll be leaving in a few days, Mel. My work's almost finished here. Then you'll have lots of time to sort things out."

Leaving? Melanie struggled to absorb the enormity of what he was saying. He was deliberately ruining their lives, making decisions for her he had no right to make, putting their happiness on hold. With a sudden, almost vicious movement, she jerked away from him and ran toward the house, blinking back a flood of tears.

"I'm sure you'll enjoy the champagne, Peter," she called out to him. "You seem to get such a kick out of bursting bubbles!"

Chapter
10

THE NEXT MORNING, Cora brought the area newspapers to Melanie's bedroom along with her breakfast tray. After spending a largely sleepless night, she was in no mood for the screaming headlines and suggestive misquotations that covered the front pages.

Pushing aside her breakfast, she read each article thoroughly, growing angrier and more worried with every paragraph. Surely one look at this pulp would clinch Peter's decision to leave.

The reporters had juiced up her comments until the stories were almost libelous, but they'd been deviously careful to stop short of printing outright lies. The result was that Melanie came off looking like either a giddy, overprotected, preening cockatoo, selfish and hedonistic, or a lonely prude who'd gullibly mistaken adventure for romance. Peter, on the other hand, was depicted as a down-on-his-luck guy who'd shared his knowledge of the world with Melanie in hopes that she would share the Carroway fortune with him!

Oh, what a complete and utter fool she'd been! How could she have ever thought she'd been in control of the press?

She stuffed the newspapers in a wastebasket and went to stand at her bedroom window, trying to think. She hadn't realized how "hot" the media considered her alleged kidnapping. And to be fair to herself, she admitted that people who were far better known than she had often been misrepresented by the press. But since Peter hadn't been present when she answered the reporters' questions in the library, he'd never believe she hadn't given them these sensational stories. How could she possibly convince him that the reporters had grossly distorted her remarks?

The door burst open, and she whirled to face Peter, who looked as if he'd eaten nails for breakfast. He stood on the threshold, a stack of newspapers under one arm, rapping one rolled-up newspaper impatiently against the door frame. "I thought you might like to start the day off with a good laugh," he said with bitter sarcasm. His voice turned cold as he read aloud the scathing headlines: "'Socialite Mixes Caviar with Pretzels'! 'Commoner Seduces Princess in Shed'! 'Is It True Love for Carroway Heiress?' 'Bodyguard Shows Heiress Difference Between Champagne and Beer'!" He spat out each headline contemptuously. "The only tidbit missing, Mel, is your explanation of how to make love during an abduction!"

She strode furiously across the room, her silk robe billowing behind her, stopping only inches from his white face. "*I* didn't write any of those headlines, Peter! And I certainly said nothing to those newsmen about our personal relationship. I didn't even mention the shed, but everyone knows that's where we were found. All some enterprising reporter had to do was to think up a suggestive way to use that information! What I resent even more than this creative journalism is your lack of faith in me! How could you even think that I'd discuss something so personal as what we meant to each other?" She closed her eyes briefly, willing the tears not to fall. Her throat and chest hurt from the burning indignation and she could no longer hold back. "You're being unfair, Peter!"

He flung the newspapers with deadly accuracy toward her bed, and seized her shoulders, forcing her to meet his piercing blue gaze. For a moment they stared unseeingly into each other's eyes, lost in their separate pain.

"You're going to find out that fame can be awfully lonely, Mel," he gritted between clenched teeth, "but what the hell? You can always sleep with your memories—they're right there in black-and-white!"

He slammed the door behind him.

By midafternoon, Melanie had worked off some of her hurt and anger by carefully analyzing Peter's behavior. He'd told her enough about his childhood to make her realize he hadn't left all of his vulnerability behind, no matter how successful he had become. Everyone was overly sensitive when it came to love, and Peter was no exception.

She knew how it felt to be rejected. She also knew what it felt like to love someone who held you up to ridicule; her marriage was a prime example of that. When she considered all of the clues left in the wake of Peter's angry withdrawal from her, they totaled up to the kind of defensive reaction she would have expected from a proud man. He felt betrayed, ignored, maybe even used. No doubt, it seemed to him that since they'd returned to the mansion he was no longer an essential part of her life, that the clamoring outside world was more important to her than he was.

Clearly she had to convince him that *he* was the center of her life, now and always. But she wasn't sure how to do that. She needed to confide in someone, receive some objective advice from a person who cared about her and her relationship with Peter. She knit her brows together, deep in thought. And then, without hesitation, she sought out her father.

She found him in the library, bent over a hundred miniature plastic soldiers that he'd arranged in strategic formations on a board designed to represent a battlefield. He glanced up distractedly as she closed the door behind her. "Oh, hullo, pet. I'm afraid I'm rather involved at the moment. You see, I'm trying to recreate a rather obscure little battle that took place in the South Pacific during the Second World War, and it's proving to be an enormously tedious task. But if I can't figure things out satisfactorily, I can't very well write about what really happened."

"I thought you were still on the Wars of the Roses," Melanie said.

Her father sighed. "I became utterly bored with that period, I'm afraid, so I decided to skip a few wars and get on with the one I remember best." He smiled, obviously pleased with himself. "I don't know why I didn't think of it sooner. It's going to shorten my book considerably."

Melanie laid a hand on his. "Father, I know how important your research is to you, but I really do need a few minutes of your undivided attention. I want to talk to you about something that's bothering me, something that's very important to my future happiness."

Worth looked momentarily bewildered, and Melanie knew he was thrown by her quiet insistence that he interrupt an activity that was sacred to him. He cleared his throat. "Well, of course, darling . . . If you're upset, I want to do everything in my power to help."

"Good," Melanie said firmly. "Come sit over here so that you won't be distracted while I talk to you."

Worth allowed himself to be led to a chair across from the love seat where Melanie sat down. She took a deep breath, trying to arrange her thoughts before she began speaking. She was surprised at how readily she'd been able to capture her father's attention. Although she knew he'd always meant to do his best by her, rarely had she been able to draw him away from his literary endeavors long enough to discuss things that really mattered to her. But she was beginning to realize she was partly to blame for not letting her father know how much she needed him. She'd given up too easily. Not this time, though.

"Father," she began, "I'm in love with Peter, and I need your advice." She explained the problem concisely, then finished by saying softly, "I don't know how to make him see that I love him for himself, not for the glimpses of life he's shown me."

Worth looked thoughtful. "Darling, I'm afraid I've been partly responsible for the way you've shut yourself off from life. In fact, I've been doing some thinking off and on since you returned from Europe. I don't imagine you would ever have married Rip if your upbringing hadn't been so overly protective. Our family chose social isolation and imposed it on you, making you afraid to take normal chances on love. No wonder you were so receptive to Rip's brand of excitement. It was a perfectly natural reaction after years of acting sensible."

He sighed, pinching the skin between his eyebrows. "I can't undo all of those years, Melanie, and I truly thought then that I was doing the right thing by you. I always depended on your practical attitude, on your making the sensible decisions needed to run the household. After your mother left us, I just couldn't bring myself to care about such details. I much preferred to work on my novel. But, pet, I didn't realize until recently that my preoccupation made me less than an effective father to you."

"Oh, Father don't blame yourself for—"

"I do, however," Worth interjected firmly. "But perhaps I can make up for some of my faults by insisting that you not let Peter Valentine slip away."

Melanie stared at him in amazement. Was her possessive and slightly dotty father telling her to go after a *man?*

"Peter Valentine's the kind of man you need," he reiterated. "Not someone like Harris, who's stuffy and dull. You mustn't settle for someone mediocre, darling. You deserve much better." He smiled pensively. "Peter's brought sunshine into this house, just as your mother did, Melanie. But Peter is reliable, where your mother wasn't. At first I failed to see her as she truly was, and made the same mistake you made with Rip. Still, I never again found the kind of joy she created. If I were to meet someone who could bring me happiness *and* be trustworthy, I'd do anything to win her heart."

Melanie blinked back tears. How incredible to be having this conversation with her father! For so long she'd been more like a parent to him than the other way around. For the first time in years, she knew the special joy of sharing with her father.

"Exactly what would you do if you were in my shoes, Father?" she asked as she rose to stand by his chair and stroke his shoulder.

He thought for a moment, absently pushing his glasses

up and down on his nose. "I'd be resourceful and daring, darling. I'd do the kinds of things that Peter himself might do if your positions were reversed. Then, after you've thoroughly captured his attention, speak from your heart. Tell him everything you've told me. Convince him that you love him."

She nodded thoughtfully. "But what if that's not enough?"

Her father grinned at her, suddenly looking ten years younger. "Don't let up on him. Be as unmerciful to him as he was to you."

That evening Melanie dressed with special care for dinner. She wanted to look her most seductive for Peter. During her bath, she thought through her plan, which would have to be as persuasive as possible to convince him that her newfound joy would be meaningless without him in her life. And what better way to do that than by reversing their positions? She was about to become the most ardent temptress in Texas.

Melanie grinned in anticipation as she replaced the simple studs she usually wore in her ears with heavy gold hoops and pulled back one side of her long hair with an ornate gold comb. She finished buttoning the sheer champagne-colored blouse, then eyed herself critically in the mirror. Not bad, she decided, turning slowly to admire the form-fitting burgundy velvet tapered slacks, which came to slightly above her ankles and were set off by her high-heeled sandals. Daringly she undid two more buttons on her blouse, offering an even better glimpse of the rounded curves of her breasts.

Mentally she reviewed the arrangements she'd made to ensure Peter's presence at dinner tonight. Even Cook had agreed to participate in the conspiracy. The crotchety woman had actually smiled as Melanie explained what she wanted her to do, throwing in an extra week of paid vacation and sealing her proposal by saying, "No, Cook, *you* won't have to deal with the mess afterward, honestly. I've already arranged for Cora to clean up."

Melanie was seated at the dining room table with the rest of the family, waiting for Cook to bring in the entrée. Peter's place next to her was conspicuously empty, just as she'd expected. He was obviously avoiding her.

She glanced around the table at her father, Aunt Maddie, and Brown, all of whom she'd carefully coached in preparation for the evening's melodrama. They'd all enthusiastically agreed to help out. Rarely had she felt such loving support from her family.

Cook entered bearing an enormous silver dish covered by a lid. She gave Melanie a surreptitious wink as she placed the dish in the center of the table and with a slow, deliberate motion, removed the lid, doused the enormous tenderloin with every last drop of a bottle of brandy, and set the meat aflame. Pandemonium broke out as fire shot into the air, creating an effect not unlike that of a small volcano erupting. The tenderloin crackled and spit noisily, spewing forth sizzling juices and filling the room with a haze of blue smoke.

"Fire! Fire! Fire!" Aunt Maddie shouted, glancing at Melanie to see if she was performing her part satisfactorily. Melanie held up two fingers. Her aunt took a deep breath, coughed on the smoke, and shouted again, "Fire! Fire!"

Worth forgot his lines as he busily tried to subdue a howling McNurty, who stood with his enormous front paws on the table, loudly grieving at the sight of the ruined meal.

Brown picked up his wineglass and downed the contents in one unrehearsed gulp before yelling, "Fire! Help!"

Cora turned from the buffet and let out a bloodcurdling scream—right on cue.

Peter made his entrance as if he, too, had studied the script. He dashed into the dining room, took one look at the conflagration, and seized a large pitcher of water from the sideboard, where Melanie had cleverly placed it. In seconds, he'd efficiently doused the flames and opened the windows to allow the smoke to escape.

Aunt Maddie fanned herself with her napkin. "Oh, my, Mr. Valentino, I don't know what we would have done without you. Cook must have poured too much brandy on the meat. We'd barely finished our soup when—poof!— the whole thing went up in flames. How fortunate for us that you heard our cries!"

Brown mumbled his line unintelligibly while sliding a

little farther down in his chair. McNurty continued to howl pathetically at well-timed intervals. Cook managed to look contrite. Cora fluttered prettily. And Worth sadly shook his head.

Peter studied the blackened tenderloin, then scanned their faces, his eyes coming to rest on Melanie's innocently pale expression, one she'd practiced for nearly an hour in the bathtub. "Are you all right?" he demanded.

"I—I think so," she returned tremulously.

"Well, I'm still quite shaken," Aunt Maddie said haughtily. "And I'd like you to stay here and protect us for the rest of this meal, Mr. Valentino. I'll feel more secure with you present. In fact, we all shall."

Worth added an emphatic, "Indeed!"

Peter reluctantly took the chair next to Melanie, as Cook carried the charred tenderloin from the room. Cora quickly replaced the sooty tablecloth with a fresh one. Melanie caught Brown's eye, and he rose to pour more wine. "Dinner will be served in a few minutes," he slurred. "Again."

"I'm sorry I didn't get here sooner," Peter apologized. "I thought I'd just have a sandwich in the basement while I made a few adjustments on Jennifer."

"Quite all right, Mr. Valentine," Melanie's father replied graciously. "But I hope we can count on your presence at dinner from now on. While you're still with us, that is. We enjoy your company, as well as your protection."

"Thank you, sir," Peter replied, looking a shade uncomfortable.

Melanie wanted to kiss her family for helping bring him back into the fold, but she knew that would have to wait until later. Conversation slowly picked up its usual, eccentric flow, although Peter remained very quiet.

Beneath the table, Melanie slipped off one shoe. As everyone continued to chat and sip wine, she slid her leg next to Peter's then edged her toes up under his pant leg. When his head snapped around in astonishment, Melanie immediately leaned slightly forward so that her blouse fell open.

His eyes darkening, he quickly turned his attention back

to the table. Melanie shifted in her chair and worked her
foot farther up his calf. His breathing became more audible.

Cook returned with a platter of something that looked
suspiciously like her infamous sandwich spread heaped into
a mound. One sprig of parsley and a single cherry garnished
the top. As Melanie put her napkin in her lap, she dropped
a hand on Peter's thigh, making him jump. *"Mel,"* he whispered in agitation, looking around to see if anyone had
noticed. No one had, of course. For once Melanie silently
blessed her family's obliviousness.

"Yes?" she asked.

"I *don't* think—"

"Well, I *have* been thinking, Peter," she cut in softly,
"and you're absolutely right. One simply can't snuggle up
to headlines."

He swallowed hard and reached for his wineglass. She
smiled with satisfaction, careful to make sure he didn't see
her. Had he repressed the memories of how he'd played this
same game with her at dinner, at the séance, or in one corner
of the mansion or another?

One thing she knew for sure; He was feeling the same
deliciously forbidden surges of desire she experienced during his sneakily sensual assaults. She could read it in his
face, hear it in his sharp intake of breath as her hand traced
a light pattern over his slacks. She could feel it in the
quivering reaction of his hard thigh muscles to her touch.

Daintily she lifted her fork to her mouth to taste the meal
Cook had just placed before her, but her other hand remained
on Peter's thigh, her foot still halfway up his calf. She
noticed he'd made no move to eat. "Aren't you hungry,
Peter?"

His eyes delved into hers. They were now such a dark
blue, they looked nearly black, reflecting his inner turmoil.
He stared at her for a few seconds before silently shaking
his head and mumbling something unintelligible. Melanie
didn't ask him to repeat it. She already knew her plan was
working.

* * *

After dessert—chocolate bars with a strange fruity topping that was Cook's specialty—Melanie followed Peter into the hall. "I'm going outside for a while, Peter. Want to come?"

He still seemed somewhat dazed from the intimate contact she'd maintained during dinner. With what appeared to be great effort, he dragged his eyes from her half-open blouse. "I told you I think we should spend less time together, Mel," he said curtly, though his voice lacked conviction.

"Hmmm...Well, that was *your* idea, not mine. I'm going outside with or without you."

"Mel, it's dark out. I don't want you wandering over the grounds unprotected at night." He sounded less sure of himself than she'd ever heard him.

She shrugged, and her breasts rose beneath the filmy material of her blouse. "There's a full moon tonight so it's not completely dark. That, along with the lighting from the terrace, ought to be enough."

He regarded her suspiciously. "Enough for what?"

"Something you introduced me to—kite flying," she answered brightly.

His expression told her he thought she'd plainly lost her wits. *"At night?"*

"They're special kites."

He folded his arms across his chest. "Mel, you can't go out by yourself after dark."

She smiled saucily. "Watch me." Before he could stop her, she picked up a large box resting next to the hall table, opened the door, and walked boldly outside. She went around the side of the house to the terrace . . . and there stood Peter waiting for her, just as she'd expected.

"What's in the box?"

"The kites, of course. I had them delivered today."

"I see."

"These are kites you can fly by moonlight," she explained. "Very romantic, not to mention fun. Don't you want to have fun, Peter?"

A variety of emotions played across his face. The last

one—surrender—remained. "Yeah . . ." He tried to sound reluctant, but Melanie knew him well enough to recognize the curiosity and desire in his voice.

She pulled two enormous kites from the box. "See? They glow in the dark; they're specially made for Halloween."

"Clever," he admitted.

Melanie suppressed a chuckle. She'd counted on his having just enough of a fun-loving spirit to be impressed with the kites. She hadn't been wrong.

They let out the strings very carefully, and before long the fluorescent kites were soaring above them, illuminated by a brilliant harvest moon. "What do you think?" she asked him.

He pretended to be studying the shadowy pattern of the tree branches across his kite, but Melanie could see she was starting to break through his reserve. "I've never seen kites like these before," he replied in what she realized was intended to be a ho-hum tone.

"When I saw the ad in the newspaper, I knew you'd love them," she said. "You were the first person I thought of."

"Really? Even with all the other things you must have on your mind—painting, partying, working on the mural for the rec center?"

"I can do all those things in my spare time, Peter. You're my main interest, and I think you know that, even if you won't admit it. I bought the kites for us to share."

He didn't answer, but his expression told her he was pleasantly surprised. It was time to push Mr. Valentine a little harder. "I'm going to run with mine," she announced casually, kicking off her shoes.

"You'll tear your stockings," he warned. "And you shouldn't get too far from the house, Mel."

"Why not? If someone is lurking in the shadows, you'll save me won't you?" She lowered her lashes. "Of course, I wouldn't *want* to be saved if that someone is you."

His scowl softened. "Mel," he said huskily, "you've got to stop this. You're driving me crazy."

Lovingly, she stroked his jaw. "You taught me everything I know about living—really living. How to make love, how to go after what I want, how to have fun. I can't turn all of that off overnight. And I don't want to. But without you, Peter, my life would be emptier than it was before, my newfound joy meaningless. Please believe me," she said softly.

He bent his head, but carefully so that her fingers remained on his cheek. Around them the shadows of the kites and leaves danced as wind ruffled through the trees. "I want to believe you, Mel," he said finally, "and I do believe that you're not responsible for the headlines. I'm sorry I blew up at you. After I calmed down, I realized those newspaper stories weren't your fault. Sometimes the press twists the facts to make a story more sensational, which is what happened to you—us . . ." He paused and when he spoke again his voice was even lower than usual. "But I still think you need more time to decide how you want to spend the rest of your life. I don't want to push you too hard, Mel. If things do happen between us, I need to know I didn't rob you of free choice."

"It's funny," Melanie replied wistfully, "but I have absolutely no scruples about doing that to you." Then, not wanting to ask for too much too soon, she thrust out one hip, withdrew her hand from his face, and said, "Now, Valentine, we're going to have a kite race. Last one to get to the moon is a rotten egg!" She began to unreel the rest of her string as she ran swiftly through the crackling leaves.

She didn't need to look over her shoulder to see what Peter was doing. She could hear him gaining on her.

The next morning, Melanie was up bright and early, planning her newest strategy. She'd had a wonderful time flying kites with Peter. They'd stayed outside half the night, enjoying the fresh air, talking about everything except their future together. However, if things went well today and tonight, Melanie figured they'd get to that subject very quickly.

It took over an hour for her to gain enough of Aunt Maddie's lucid attention to feel confident that she'd play the role assigned her this morning with a good measure of credibility. After Melanie finished coaching her aunt, she went to look for Brown, who was obviously feeling no pain. She asked him to groom McNurty, praying he could stay on his feet long enough to finish the job.

When Brown finally stumbled into the kitchen with McNurty in tow, Melanie breathed a sigh of relief. The dog's thick brown coat stuck out in uneven tufts and patches, thanks to Brown's bumbling efforts with the electric clipper. Perfect, Melanie decided. This was a crisis that demanded Peter's assistance.

Aunt Maddie let out a genuine gasp of dismay when she saw the dog. "Oh, my, Melanie, you really think this is going to turn out all right? I mean, I want to help you with Mr. Valentino, but I just don't know . . ."

Melanie patted her aunt's hand. "It's going to be wonderful. McNurty will look fine when Peter and I finish with him. Better than ever." She paused, trying to think of something else that would reassure her aunt. "By the time he's completely groomed, McNurty will be ready to pose for a portrait that will be more smashing than any of his predecessors."

Aunt Maddie smiled hopefully, beginning to look a little relieved. "I'm sure you're right, Melanie, and I've explained the entire situation to McNurty. He has his part down to a tee." She waved her hand in dismissal at Brown, who gladly staggered out the door. Then she leaned conspiratorially toward Melanie. "Is now the time to lure Mr. Valentino in here, dear?"

Melanie nodded. "If your handkerchief's ready, Aunt, so am I."

Aunt Maddie took a deep breath as if she were going to break into a song, but instead, she burst into tears—loud, gasping sobs that couldn't be stifled by the lace handkerchief she clutched to her mouth. Melanie put an arm around her, which is how Peter found them when he came running up from the basement.

"What the devil—!" He stopped dead in his tracks, staring past a weeping Aunt Maddie and a consoling Melanie to McNurty, who sat dejectedly in a far corner of the kitchen, regarding the ruins of his shaggy brown coat. He resembled a moth-eaten hearth rug—and an extremely unattractive one at that.

"Good Lord! What happened to McNurty?" Peter gasped.

Melanie led Aunt Maddie to the table and urged her to sit. "Brown groomed him," she answered simply.

Peter gaped at McNurty. "Brown did *this?*"

Melanie sighed. "Aunt wanted McNurty groomed in preparation for the portrait I plan to do of him, but now . . ." She gestured helplessly toward the dog, who, as if on cue, howled despairingly.

Aunt Maddie slowly took the handkerchief away from her face. "Oh, Mr. Valentino, Brown's made a terrible mess of my gorgeous McNurty. You must help us!"

Peter looked at Melanie who drew her aunt a little closer. "Aunt's so upset, I don't know what to do."

Peter jammed his hands in his pockets. "Well, of course, I want to help, but what in the world can *I* do?" Aunt Maddie opened her mouth to offer her rehearsed suggestion, but Peter suddenly withdrew a hand from his pocket and snapped his fingers. "I know! I could arrange to take McNurty to a professional groomer! I'll go call—"

"No!" Melanie and Aunt Maddie shouted in unison.

Peter regarded them curiously.

"McNurty doesn't—" Melanie began, floundering.

"Like cars," Aunt Maddie finished, sniffing. Melanie shot her an admiring glance. She had really thrown herself into the role, but then, her aunt had had years of practice acting out different characters in her father's novel.

Peter spread his palms. "Well, then, I don't know what the solution is. Unless . . . maybe we could arrange for a professional groomer to come here."

Aunt Maddie peered over the edge of her lace handkerchief. "A-actually, McNurty h-had a very bad experience w-with a professional groomer once," she hiccuped. More forcefully, she added, "But I think I might have an idea. You and Melanie could give McNurty a fancy poodle clip. You know, the kind with little round puffs on the legs and hips, and a ruff at the neck."

Peter looked as if someone had just suggested he become a snake charmer. *"A poodle clip!* Good Lord! McNurty doesn't look *anything* like a poodle. He looks like a . . . a gas station dog!"

Aunt Maddie began to cry harder. Melanie turned a pleading glance on Peter. "Please, Peter. You and I are the only ones who are up to managing this. Aunt's heart seems to be set on giving McNurty a poodle clip, and I don't think she should be fooling around with scissors and an electric clipper." She smiled meaningfully at him. "She might cut herself. Besides, we'll have fun doing it, and it would help the family out of a jam."

He stared at her incredulously, but she could tell her remark about her aunt fooling around with scissors had made an impression on him. His gaze traveled to McNurty, whose ears went down on cue. Slowly, Peter's mouth curved into a smile, which he quickly covered with the back of his hand. He seemed to be deliberating. Finally he recovered himself enough to say, "All right, if you really think I can be of some help."

Melanie ran over to kiss him exuberantly on the cheek. "Oh, thanks, Peter! I told Aunt Maddie you'd help us out of this predicament. Now, why don't you take Aunt to her room, and by the time you get back, I'll have everything ready to begin working on McNurty."

Three hours later, Peter and Melanie escorted a prancing McNurty into the library, where Aunt Maddie, Brown and Worth awaited the results of their endeavors.

"Oh, darlings, he looks wonderful!" Aunt Maddie rushed over to embrace McNurty, who was preening shamelessly in a clip that featured heart-shaped puffs of fluffy hair on his back and sides and an elaborately scalloped ruff around his neck. "Why, Melanie, with this lovely teased pompadour between his ears, he actually looks like Harold," Aunt Maddie cooed. "When Harold was really Harold, that is. Don't you think so, Worth?"

Worth adjusted his spectacles and bent closer to the McNurty in question, then replied, "Indeed. Perhaps even a slight improvement. As I recall, the original Harold McNurty had a receding hairline, which is not the case with this one."

Brown sniffed, his nostrils flaring in disgust. "McNurty seems to be wearing *perfume!*"

"It's not perfume, exactly," Melanie explained. "It's a special hair spray made for dogs. I think it smells wonderful, Brown, but it'll wear off in a day or two, which should please you."

"Very well. But until it does, he may not sit next to me at the dinner table."

Aunt Maddie ignored the cantankerous butler. "Melanie, was it very difficult to give McNurty this clip?"

"Not really. I did the hearts, and Peter did the scallops."

"Actually," Peter began solemnly, "the biggest problem was deciding whether to use rose- or carnation-scented hair spray."

Worth nodded gravely. "I can well imagine."

McNurty swaggered across the room and began to dance in excited circles around the group. Melanie smiled delightedly. McNurty was ecstatic over his new look, and she and Peter had worked well together, joking, laughing, playing with the silly dog, enjoying the challenge, and at the same time happily solving the family crisis. Whether Peter realized it or not, they'd also been slowly putting the pieces of their own relationship back together, exactly what she'd hoped would happen.

McNurty suddenly sat down next to Brown, rubbing against his leg. The butler held his nose and muttered grumpily, "Perhaps next time you might use musk or lavender spray, or perhaps lime or jasmine . . ."

Peter exchanged an amused glance with Melanie and drew her close. "I love this family," he said softly.

She snuggled into the curve of his arm. "Me, too," she agreed wholeheartedly. "Me, too."

The next day, Melanie sat down at the dressing table in her room and rang the number of the local Salvation Army office. She spent a few moments explaining that she would like to make a large contribution in exchange for a certain item they had in stock. Having satisfactorily arranged the trade, she called one of the most exclusive stores in Fort Worth and asked to speak with Miss Campbell, the matronly saleslady who for years had selected clothes for Melanie and delivered them to her home.

Melanie greeted the saleslady warmly and explained why she was calling. "Miss Campbell, I saw your newspaper ad for—"

"Ah, yes, dear. A brand-new shipment just arrived. Some perfectly divine lightweight wool blazers and marvelously tailored suits. You know, earth tones in subtle tweeds and pinstripes—the kind of garments that constitute an essential part of the conservative woman's wardrobe. Shall I send out a selection for you to choose from?"

"That's not the ad I was referring to, Miss Campbell," Melanie corrected her. "I'm interested in the collection of jungle lingerie."

There was a long pause. "I see. For a gift, dear?"

"I suppose it is—in a way. I'd like you to send out the chiffon leopard-print negligee as soon as possible, please. It's imperative that I have it by tonight."

Another pregnant pause followed. Then Miss Campbell finally managed to say, "Well, of course, if that's what you'd like, but I must warn you that this garment is nothing like anything else you have in your wardrobe, Miss Carroway, and I'm afraid you'll be very disappointed. Perhaps you couldn't tell from the photograph, dear, but it's hardly a conservative number."

"Oh, I could tell, Miss Campbell," Melanie reassured her. "And that's exactly why it appeals to me. Send it out immediately in my size, please."

The clock in the hall struck eleven as Melanie glided toward Peter's bedroom, wearing an olive-green rubber raincoat. She paused only an instant before knocking softly. Within seconds, she heard footsteps inside the Tropical Paradise Room; then the door opened and she was staring into Peter's surprised eyes.

"Good Lord, Mel, why do you have on—?"

She flew past him and seized a thick macramé room divider that an enterprising decorator, given full creative rein, had hung like a vine from the sturdy overhead beams. Pulling the "vine" with her, she backed across the length of the large room, then ran swiftly forward, wrapping her feet around the vine and flying through the air. Peter gaped as she landed directly in front of him with a barely discernible thump. "Hi," she said sexily.

"Mel—?" Peter combed his fingers through his hair, but the tumbled waves settled immediately back into their usual casual style—thick, full, and enticingly touchable. He was wearing nothing but faded jeans that clung to his muscular thighs, and the dim light spilling from the hall danced over his bronzed chest and powerful shoulders.

"Why don't you think of me as . . . Jane?" she suggested seductively, "and yourself as Tarzan?"

Peter stared at her. "I didn't know Jane wore a rubber raincoat," he remarked dryly, quietly closing the door.

Melanie looked down from her vine in pretended horror. "Oh, my. I completely forgot. You see, I had this on when the boat capsized in that awful storm. Luckily, we weren't too far from shore." With a flourish, she unsnapped the front of the Salvation Army raincoat. "This made wonderful camouflage," she explained, "Helped me blend in with the foliage so wild beasts didn't notice me so readily. But I feel perfectly safe in this part of the jungle." Slowly, she slipped out of the raincoat, which fell to her bare feet.

Peter caught his breath in a guttural gasp. "Good Lord, Mel, what—?"

She lowered her lashes, turning around to give him a complete view of the scandalously revealing negligee. Made of nearly transparent gold chiffon, it was a perfect complement to her auburn hair. Fashioned like an outfit that Jane might have worn with Tarzan, it was held in place by only one strap that ran crosswise over her left shoulder and a black silk cord around her waist. The skirt rested high on her thighs, its hem cut in a jagged line, allowing tempting glimpses of ivory skin. But the gown's most startling feature was strategically placed satin appliqués shaped like the spots of a leopard.

"Y-you shouldn't be here, Mel." Peter's breathing was ragged as his eyes traveled over her.

"I know," she said resignedly. "But it's not my fault I found myself . . . at sea tonight. I'm the only survivor of the shipwreck—just as you're the only other human being on this tropical island." She trailed a finger down his rapidly rising and falling chest.

"Mel, we're not going to make love," he informed her. "I think that would. . ." Melanie's finger circled his navel just above the low-riding waistband of his jeans. "Complicate things," he finished hoarsely.

"I'm sure you're right, Peter." Her gaze shifted around the room which was just as she remembered it. The wall behind the bed was papered in a bold print of banana leaves and palm fronds. The other walls were covered in grass cloth. A lamp with a monkey-shaped base burned next to the enormous bed, spilling light onto the rattan headboard and yellow-orange satin comforter. The rest of the furniture was made of cane and upholstered in tiger-gold and lime-green silk. The windows were open slightly, and curtains made of mosquito netting fluttered in the cool night breeze. The carpeting was the color of sun-bleached sand and thickly luxuriant beneath her bare feet.

"The Tropical Paradise Room has never looked more beautiful," she murmured, walking over to sit down on the edge of the bed.

Peter jammed his hands into his pockets, eyeing her warily. "I thought you told me once that you don't care for it."

"I can't imagine why I ever said such a thing," she protested. "This room is full of exotic imagery, sensual symbolism . . ." Her eyes didn't leave his face as she assumed a languid pose, stretching out on the bed and leaning back on an elbow with one leg bent at an alluring angle. "So . . . what do you think of my outfit, Peter?" she asked, tossing her long hair over a bare shoulder.

His eyes became glazed as they took in the satin markings

that just managed to conceal her nipples and the V-shaped area between her thighs. Melanie shifted slightly, and the rest of the gauzy, see-through fabric shimmered in the pale light. He groaned, closing his eyes briefly. Then they flickered slowly open. "Mel, I hope you know how hard you're making this for me. You're so beautiful . . ."

"Why don't we just talk, Peter?" she suggested softly, beckoning for him to join her on the bed.

He shook his head. "I don't think that would be such a good idea."

She patted a spot at the foot of the bed. "Oh, it won't hurt you to keep me company for a little while. Just the two of us talking quietly." Her voice was as breathy as a balmy breeze on a tropical night.

He moved slowly toward her and sat gingerly on the foot of the bed, his restless gaze raking her body. "What did you want to talk about?"

"Whatever," she returned airily. She leaned back on both elbows, letting the gown's spots move out of position, revealing the pouting tips of her breasts and the shadowy triangle far below. Casually she lifted a bare foot and ran it along his jean-clad thigh. "This room offers limitless possibilities . . ." He swallowed hard. "For intimate conversation . . ." Her foot slid up his bare chest, her toes weaving through the thick mat of curly golden hair. She smiled knowingly. "Don't you think?" Her toe gently flicked a nipple.

A groan tore from Peter's throat as he moved quickly to cover her body with his own. One of his legs inserted itself between her thighs; the other braced against the bed to keep his full weight from descending on her. He stared down into her face with eyes that had turned dark blue-green, like turbulent waters in the midst of a hurricane. "It's hard to talk when you're being buffeted by a storm," he murmured.

She reached up to caress his face, allowing her head to fall back against his bent elbow. The rigid line of his jaw had relaxed slightly, she noted, and his expression no longer revealed his obvious efforts at self-control. "Communication," she reminded him, "can take many forms . . ."

He continued to run his eyes over her slender curves. Slowly the shivery feeling in her limbs was replaced by a hot blaze that consumed her inner being. Abruptly he rolled onto his back, lifting his hips a few inches off the bed as he stripped off his jeans and undershorts.

He knelt beside her on the bed, one hand resting at her waist, his fingers playing with the black silk cord. Wordlessly he undid the tie and tossed it to one side. Melanie waited breathlessly until he lowered the strap on her shoulder, sliding the gown down her body. She lay completely naked atop the kumquat-colored comforter, surrounded by a tropical paradise.

As if in slow motion, Peter bent to kiss each breast, capturing the throbbing nipples with his mouth. Her fingers tangled in his hair and moved down to mold the rippling muscles of his shoulders. He rose above her, trapping her for an instant in his flashing gaze. "I need you so much," she murmured. *"You're* the magic in my life, Peter. Now, always."

His response was to feather a hot trail of kisses down her throat, over her breasts, and on to her navel, where his tongue dipped maddeningly before it continued a tantalizing path . . . lower and lower. Melanie gasped aloud, straining upward for more of the sweet agony. Her head tossed back and forth restlessly as she arched her hips. Her eyes opened wider as Peter's tongue followed a sensual path along her inner thigh, lapping over her hot skin like the surge of a torrid ocean wave, like the sun-warmed spill of a waterfall deep in the heart of the jungle.

She ran her hands over his sleek tanned body, the corded muscles of his back, the trim expanse of his waist, and the sinewy area where hip joined thigh. Then, unable to withstand the exquisite tactile exploration of his marvelous ministrations any longer, she spread her hands over his hips, urging him to come to her.

His head lifted slowly from one of her long legs. Then his hands caught her shoulders, and with an easy agility, he flipped them over gracefully, exchanging their positions. Gently he guided her onto him, his long, supple fingers fanning along the curve of her spine, then beneath her hips, slowly pulling her downward.

She shuddered, keenly aware of these new sensations and pleasures, eager to increase their intensity. With a fierce, rocking motion, she abandoned herself completely, plunging recklessly on and on . . .

When release came, she threw back her head. Beneath her, Peter rose to cross the last barrier between them, echoing her pleasure-filled cry. They prolonged the ecstasy for as long as possible, soaring above themselves, breathing deeply of the air's musky scent, until all sights and sounds became one, and Melanie collapsed on Peter's chest. They lay exhausted for an incalculable time, lungs heaving, limp-limbed.

Finally Peter rolled her gently onto her side, cradling her in the curve of his arm.

"I told you the Tropical Paradise Room would be conducive to articulate expression," she murmured.

"Must be the mosquito netting," he replied huskily. "Of course, when Jane showed up to seduce Tarzan so cunningly—"

"Peter! Do you really think I wanted anything more than your . . . company?"

"Oh, yeah," he drawled lazily. "I sure as hell do."

"You could have asked me to leave," she pointed out blithely.

"Hmmm . . . That's what I intended to do when I sat on the bed. But I'm a kind man, basically, and how do you tell a beautiful shipwreck survivor to call a cab and go home?" The slightest hint of a smile played about his lips. "Tonight you've effectively destroyed my rather well-earned reputation as a street-smart guy, Mel. A man disciplined in nearly every aspect of life. And you did it all with a rubber raincoat and a flimsy piece of chiffon that wouldn't cover a gnat."

"I won't tell any of your employees," she teased, stroking a lock of hair back from his still damp forehead. Her tone turned serious. "I love you, Peter, and no amount of time in the world will ever change that fact."

One strong hand lifted to cup the nape of her neck as he smiled his familiar smile, the one that had always seemed especially created for her. "Mel..."

"Hmmm?"

"Do you think you could convince me a little more?"

"Oh, yes," she breathed. "A little, a lot, forever."

Chapter

11

MELANIE LEFT THE Tropical Paradise Room shortly after the sun rose, feeling absolutely exhilarated, despite her lack of sleep. She and Peter had made love repeatedly during the night, each time coming together more slowly and tenderly. It was as if, after the initial blaze of passion, the fire still burned as brightly, but they were able to enjoy its warmth at their leisure. She had every confidence she'd changed Peter's mind about waiting awhile before they made a definite commitment to each other. But just to make sure, she would proceed with her grand finale. The arrangements were somewhat complicated, and she sat down at her dressing table to make a careful check-list of last-minute details.

By early afternoon, she had finished all of the phone calls needed to put her plan into motion. She took a long bath and dressed carefully in a magenta slacks set, allowing her hair to casually frame her face. Then she went to find Peter.

He was in the downstairs hall, about to enter the library. His senses alerted him to her presence before she even spoke. His face broke into a smile. "You look wonderful, Mel. I like your outfit, although I liked the one last night even better."

She hurried down the last few stairs and threw her arms

around his neck. *"You're* the only one who'll ever get a chance to appreciate my leopard outfit, Peter."

His expression was tender as he said quietly, "I really have overreacted a lot lately, Mel. Probably because I feel as if I've been caught in a fairy tale in which I rescued a beautiful princess from the tower and she turned out to be merely grateful—nothing more . . ."

"I'm not a princess, Peter," she reassured him. "I'm a real woman with real feelings, and I won't vanish into thin air or run off into the kingdom to sample all of its delights. I want only a life with you."

His eyes caught the late-afternoon sunshine streaming through the narrow windows. Melanie gazed into their sparkling depths and found herself drowning in them for the hundredth time since she'd come to know this fascinating, complex man. His head inclined slightly. "I do love you, you know, Mel," he said tenderly. "I love you very much."

Something deep inside her gave an odd little tug as he said the magic words. Their lips met in a kiss that told her he no longer had any doubts of her love for him.

A loud whirring noise outside interrupted their embrace. "What the hell—?" Peter exclaimed. The library door flew open and Worth, Aunt Maddie, Brown, and McNurty rushed into the hall.

"Stay in the house!" Peter ordered, throwing open the front door and running onto the lawn. Paying no attention to his command, the family trooped outside after him.

Three helicopters hovered over the grounds. Peter was staring up at them, his face a mixture of puzzlement and concern. Melanie hurried to his side, but he seized her arm and turned her back toward the mansion. "Honey, get inside!" he warned. "I don't know what's—"

He never got a chance to finish his sentence. Suddenly dozens of huge, brightly colored balloons were released from the helicopters. They floated along the tops of the trees, a rainbow sea against a background of rich russets and golds. Some of the balloons were shaped like hearts; others resembled wedding rings. But they all had one thing in common. Gleaming foil letters marched across each one, spelling out the words: BE MINE, VALENTINE!

Peter's hand dropped from Melanie's arm as his eyes tracked the flight of the balloons across the blue-gray sky. He turned slowly to her. "Mel, this is the most spectacular way of making a point."

Behind them on the front steps Aunt Maddie was clapping, and her father was shouting, "Bravo!" McNurty lumbered across the lawn, his scalloped ruff bouncing smartly. Brown's voice, somewhat slurred as usual, mumbled phrases that Melanie suspected were supposed to be jubilant, though it was hard to tell from his monotone.

She threw her arms around an incredulous Peter. "Hard to believe a sensible girl would go to these lengths, isn't it?" she asked mischievously.

He passed a hand over his eyes, then looked at her with such love and tenderness, she felt a lump rise in her throat. Around them, the balloons continued to bob gently on the breeze, even as the helicopters sputtered across the sky, the whir of their rotors fading into the distance.

"I love you, Mel," Peter breathed, his hands sliding to the small of her back. Her arms remained around his neck and they stood, oblivious to everyone and everything except each other.

Melanie rained kisses over Peter's bronzed cheek, inhaling the scent of him, adoring the feel of his hard muscles pressed into her soft curves. "Well, will you?" she asked softly.

He was drinking in the sight of her. "Will I what?" he murmured vaguely.

She withdrew one arm from his neck and gestured toward the closest balloon, a hot-pink heart with bright red foil letters. "Be mine, Valentine?" she whispered.

He pretended to ponder the question, his features losing some of their intensity as his mouth broke into a teasing smile. "I'll have to ask you some very important questions of my own first," he cautioned playfully.

"I warn you that I'll cheat to come up with the right answers."

"Lord, I hope so. Now, Mel, how do you feel about a wedding cake topped with anchovies?"

"I love it."

"And since McNurty looks so trendy in his unique clip, I think he should be in the wedding party, don't you agree?"

"Absolutely."

"And about the honeymoon..."

She ran her fingers through his thick, shining hair. "There's only one place I'd consider spending our wedding night, Peter."

He smiled knowingly. She smiled back, and they said in unison, "The shed."

As another heart-shaped balloon floated by, Peter caught its string and in one deft motion tied it around Melanie's ring finger.

That got a round of applause from the porch. Aunt Maddie called out, "Darling, I'm going to love your new name. Melanie Valentino. It's so romantic."

"Indeed," Worth agreed.

"Quite," Brown echoed.

"How soon can we get married?" Peter asked huskily.

"Does waiting until tomorrow seem too *sensible?*"

He caressed her face lovingly. "Yes, but it's going to take a little time to have the wedding cake made, Mel, not to mention airing McNurty out thoroughly before we mist him with orange-blossom hair spray. So I suppose we'll just have to figure out a way to fill in the hours until then... somehow..."

"I have a suggestion," she returned, motioning for him to put his ear next to her mouth.

Peter listened for a few seconds, then enfolded her in his arms. "Meet you in the Tropical Paradise Room around eleven tonight, Mel. And don't bother to wear the raincoat ... or the spots."

SECOND CHANCE AT LOVE

COMING NEXT MONTH

SWANN'S SONG #334 by Carole Buck
Knowing both karate and kids, Megan Harper poses
as a nanny to secretly guard rock star Colin Swann and
his irrepressible son...and gets into deep
trouble when love complicates the deception!

STOLEN KISSES #335 by Liz Grady
Mattie Hamilton is rehearsing a museum
heist when tuxedo-clad thief Devlin Seamus Devlin
tackles her in midair...and offers to tutor
her in *all* kinds of midnight maneuvers!

GOLDEN GIRL #336 by Jacqueline Topaz
In sophisticated Hollywood, schoolteacher Olivia Gold
finds both her movie star grandmother *and* dashing soulmate
Andrew Carr—who transforms her into a glittering
golden girl and spellbinds her with sensual enchantment.

SMILES OF A SUMMER NIGHT #337 by Delaney Devers
Like a modern rogue, plantation owner
Jules Robichaux sweeps April Jasper away with cynical
charm, smoothly seduces her under moonlit
magnolias...but won't trust her enough to offer his love.

DESTINY'S DARLING #338 by Adrienne Edwards
"Bought" by ex-husband Bart Easton at a charity
benefit, Dot Biancardi recalls poignant moments—of
gallant courtship, wedded bliss...and lonely
heartache. Dare she risk repeating past mistakes?

WILD AND WONDERFUL #339 by Lee Williams
Trapped on a wild Maine island with brawny recluse
Greg Bowles, who's rejected the inheritance she's come to
give him, heir hunter Alicia Saunders finds a new
tension building...desire quickening.

SECOND CHANCE AT LOVE

Be Sure to Read These New Releases!

BELONGING TO TAYLOR #322 by Kay Robbins
Taylor Shannon employs her mindreading
talents, psychic family, peculiar pets, and sexy
satins to lure gallant but reluctant Trevor
King, then pursues him until he catches her!

ANYWHERE AND ALWAYS #323 by Lee Williams
Brilliant inventor Justin Fuller, an Albert
Einstein and offbeat Romeo in one explosively sensual
package, dazzles Lydie Henley with high-tech
wizardry and X-rated kisses...but makes no promises.

FORTUNE'S CHOICE #324 by Elissa Curry
Destitute socialite "Joey" Fortune
and dashing ne'er-do-well Nick Parmenter join
forces to recoup their losses by selling ice
cream...and discover sweet love.

LADY ON THE LINE #325 by Cait Logan
Arrogantly chauvinistic one moment, hot and
tender the next, Barrett Redding is almost more man than
K.C. Bollins can handle—especially when his underlying
vulnerability threatens to crush her last resistance!

A KISS AWAY #326 by Sherryl Woods
With her fortieth birthday approaching, Jessica
Warren tries—but fails—to resist erotically roguish Kevin
Lawrence, whose playfulness and gleaming pectorals
utterly undermine her sense of what's proper...

PLAY IT AGAIN, SAM #327 by Petra Diamond
When brash Hollywood designer Sam
Harrison invades nostalgic Nedda Shaw's sleepy
Southern town, she's too bollixed to
distinguish between a summer fling and lasting love.

Order on opposite page

SECOND CHANCE AT LOVE

___ 0-425-08627-5	SPRING MADNESS #299 Aimée Duvall	$2.25
___ 0-425-08628-3	SIREN'S SONG #300 Linda Barlow	$2.25
___ 0-425-08629-1	MAN OF HER DREAMS #301 Katherine Granger	$2.25
___ 0-425-08630-5	UNSPOKEN LONGINGS #302 Dana Daniels	$2.25
___ 0-425-08631-3	THIS SHINING HOUR #303 Antonia Tyler	$2.25
___ 0-425-08672-0	THE FIRE WITHIN #304 Laine Allen	$2.25
___ 0-425-08673-9	WHISPERS OF AN AUTUMN DAY #305 Lee Williams	$2.25
___ 0-425-08674-7	SHADY LADY #306 Jan Mathews	$2.25
___ 0-425-08675-5	TENDER IS THE NIGHT #307 Helen Carter	$2.25
___ 0-425-08676-3	FOR LOVE OF MIKE #308 Courtney Ryan	$2.25
___ 0-425-08677-1	TWO IN A HUDDLE #309 Diana Morgan	$2.25
___ 0-425-08749-1	LOVERS AND PRETENDERS #310 Liz Grady	$2.25
___ 0-425-08750-6	SWEETS TO THE SWEET #311 Jeanne Grant	$2.25
___ 0-425-08751-4	EVER SINCE EVE #312 Kasey Adams	$2.25
___ 0-425-08752-2	BLITHE SPIRIT #313 Mary Haskell	$2.25
___ 0-425-08753-0	MAN AROUND THE HOUSE #314 Joan Darling	$2.25
___ 0-425-08754-9	DRIVEN TO DISTRACTION #315 Jamisan Whitney	$2.25
___ 0-425-08850-2	DARK LIGHTNING #316 Karen Keast	$2.25
___ 0-425-08851-0	MR. OCTOBER #317 Carole Buck	$2.25
___ 0-425-08852-9	ONE STEP TO PARADISE #318 Jasmine Craig	$2.25
___ 0-425-08853-7	TEMPTING PATIENCE #319 Christina Dair	$2.25
___ 0-425-08854-5	ALMOST LIKE BEING IN LOVE #320 Betsy Osborne	$2.25
___ 0-425-08855-3	ON CLOUD NINE #321 Jean Kent	$2.25
___ 0-425-08908-8	BELONGING TO TAYLOR #322 Kay Robbins	$2.25
___ 0-425-08909-6	ANYWHERE AND ALWAYS #323 Lee Williams	$2.25
___ 0-425-08910-X	FORTUNE'S CHOICE #324 Elissa Curry	$2.25
___ 0-425-08911-8	LADY ON THE LINE #325 Cait Logan	$2.25
___ 0-425-08948-7	A KISS AWAY #326 Sherryl Woods	$2.25
___ 0-425-08949-5	PLAY IT AGAIN, SAM #327 Petra Diamond	$2.25
___ 0-425-08966-5	SNOWFLAME #328 Christa Merlin	$2.25
___ 0-425-08967-3	BRINGING UP BABY #329 Diana Morgan	$2.25
___ 0-425-08968-1	DILLON'S PROMISE #330 Cinda Richards	$2.25
___ 0-425-08969-X	BE MINE, VALENTINE #331 Hilary Cole	$2.25
___ 0-425-08970-3	SOUTHERN COMFORT #332 Kit Windham	$2.25
___ 0-425-08971-1	NO PLACE FOR A LADY #333 Cassie Miles	$2.25